SPECIAL MESSAGE TO READERS

THE ULVERSCROFT FOUNDATION
(registered UK charity number 264873)

was established in 1972 to provide funds for research, diagnosis and treatment of eye diseases. Examples of major projects funded by the Ulverscroft Foundation are:-

- The Children's Eye Unit at Moorfields Eye Hospital, London
- The Ulverscroft Children's Eye Unit at Great Ormond Street Hospital for Sick Children
- Funding research into eye diseases and treatment at the Department of Ophthalmology, University of Leicester
- The Ulverscroft Vision Research Group, Institute of Child Health
- Twin operating theatres at the Western Ophthalmic Hospital, London
- The Chair of Ophthalmology at the Royal Australian College of Ophthalmologists

You can help further the work of the Foundation by making a donation or leaving a legacy. Every contribution is gratefully received. If you would like to help support the Foundation or require further information, please contact:

THE ULVERSCROFT FOUNDATION
The Green, Bradgate Road, Anstey
Leicester LE7 7FU, England
Tel: (0116) 236 4325

website: www.foundation.ulverscroft.com

LOST AND FOUND

Ex-nautical engineer turned treasure hunter Alex Harding is about to embark on a salvage operation in the Caribbean, hunting for booty from a sunken ship. Auctioneer Zoe hopes to gain exclusive auction rights to his finds for her company. They're immediately attracted to each other, but Alex seems to be involved with Maria, and Zoe doesn't want to end up with a womanizer. There's more than buried bullion at stake — love is also up for the asking. But who will win the final bid?

Books by Wendy Kremer
in the Linford Romance Library:

REAP THE WHIRLWIND
AT THE END OF THE RAINBOW
WHERE BLUEBELLS GROW WILD
WHEN WORDS GET IN THE WAY
COTTAGE IN THE COUNTRY
WAITING FOR A STAR TO FALL
SWINGS AND ROUNDABOUTS
KNAVE OF DIAMONDS
SPADES AND HEARTS
TAKING STEPS
I'LL BE WAITING
HEARTS AND CRAFTS
THE HEART SHALL CHOOSE
THE HOUSE OF RODRIGUEZ
WILD FRANGIPANI
TRUE COLOURS
A SUMMER IN TUSCANY

WENDY KREMER

♦

LOST AND FOUND

Complete and Unabridged

LINFORD
Leicester

First published in Great Britain in 2014

First Linford Edition
published 2015

*A catalogue record for this book is available
from the British Library.*

ISBN 978–1–4448–2586–2

Published by
F. A. Thorpe (Publishing)
Anstey, Leicestershire

Set by Words & Graphics Ltd.
Anstey, Leicestershire
Printed and bound in Great Britain by
T. J. International Ltd., Padstow, Cornwall

This book is printed on acid-free paper

1

'What makes you think I need your money?' Alex Harding leaned back, the chair creaking softly under his weight. His pale grey eyes assessed her carefully. He recognized the challenge in her expression and liked it.

Zoe Michener eyed him. He didn't sound encouraging, and she wondered how she could persuade him. Ignoring the possibility of setback, she said, 'Surely extra money is always welcome.' Zoe had naively expected he'd just grab the money and be grateful. The task was more difficult than she expected. 'Why dismiss it off-hand? It's worth thinking about, isn't it?'

He studied her for a moment. 'Sometimes extra money is good . . . but sometimes it makes everything more complicated. It means too many people feel they're entitled to interfere and ask too many questions. I don't want, or need, that kind of hassle.'

Her eyes widened and she hurried to reassure him. 'I promise you, Williams & Co. won't interfere. We just hope you'll give us one concession if we invest.'

He lifted his brows and his tone sounded brusque and business-like. 'And what's that? No one knows if we'll find anything.' He shifted and continued, 'In fact you'd be better off investing your cash in gilt-edged securities.'

A waitress deposited their cups of coffee. Zoe noticed how she eyed Alex Harding. Zoe automatically eyed him more closely too, and agreed with the other woman's approving glance. Physically he was a very attractive man, and she judged him to be intelligent and dynamic. She also had a feeling he'd already sized her up.

Zoe hoped she didn't sound too tenacious. 'We know there's a risk, and we accept that. We only want one thing:

the right to auction anything you find. We understand nothing about salvaging or treasure hunting, so we won't meddle in how you conduct your search.'

He eyed her warily but his expression was more relaxed. There was a long pause, and she almost thought she'd lost, but then he surprised her and asked, 'What kind of money are we talking about?'

Sounding more confident than she felt, she replied, 'Ten thousand.'

Something like amusement flickered in his eyes. 'You really don't have a clue about what's involved, do you? A venture of this kind takes a lot of money. The ship cost a small fortune, and I needed more money for special equipment. That was when my crew agreed to invest their savings. In other words, I don't need any more investors.'

Zoe moistened her lips. 'But our participation would provide you with a back-up fund for unforeseen snags.' Her face remained expressionless even though her brain was whizzing into top gear. She studied him as she waited for his reaction and tried to anticipate his reply. Silence hung between them again. Perhaps he was merely fishing for more. Was he haggling and hoping she'd increase her offer? Zoe wouldn't wring any more out of William Williams, head of the company. It had taken all her persuasive powers to get this much. For some stupid reason, silliness triumphed over common sense in her brain. She was sure this idea would work. She fingered her bag at her side and stared across the table at his sunburned face. She'd been saving for a couple of years for emergencies.

He interrupted her thoughts. 'There's no guarantee that any of us will ever see their money again. It's a risk — a calculated one, but it's still a risk. Success or failure is an equal possibility. The crew know me, and they know I'd never intentionally cheat them. I've never heard of your company. You don't know much about me either.'

'I know enough. I've checked you out via the internet, and Tony vouches for you. I heard about your plans through him. We don't intend to interfere, or bombard you with reproaches if it fails. We realize there's a risk.' She took a deep breath. 'I think, now that I've met you, that I can even persuade my company to double the amount to twenty thousand. We're mainly interested in the right to auction the finds. Getting our money back, plus a profit, would be brilliant of course, but it's not why we want to be part of it. Auctioning rights are what we're after.' Despite her effort not to show nerves, Zoe's cheeks were bright pink as she considered his face and its inherent strength. He was a forceful character, but so was she.

Alex didn't need the money, but her attitude and intensity interested him more than he cared to admit. Her single-minded attitude didn't lessen her femininity; it merely increased his interest. The fact that she'd arranged to meet him via Tony, and didn't just take his initial 'no' for an answer, showed she had spirit. He straightened, met her glance, and said firmly, 'Okay! I'll consider it and let you know.'

He had a sneaking suspicion she was very nervous, but she hid it well. Her auburn hair glistened like polished wood and her eyes were a mixture of amber and green. He'd met quite a number of attractive women in his life, and she was very attractive. Beautiful was going too far, but she looked good. She had an inviting figure that curved in the right places, and he eyed her conventional clothes, expensive wrist-watch, high cheekbones, almond-shaped eyes, and delicate skin with approval. He'd deliberately avoided meaningful relationships ever since Diana had tripped him up. For a moment he thought seriously about angling for a date, but then decided against it. Her attitude was too conservative. She was a straight-down-the-road type of woman who expected commitment and faithfulness. That was a no-go area for him these days. He just needed hassle-free relationships with no strings attached.

He took a sip of coffee. 'That's your main requirement? Exclusive auctioning rights?'

Zoe viewed him confidently, even though she still felt uneasy. He was deeply tanned. His hair was sun-bleached, thick and tousled. It needed trimming. He had prominent bones and his most attractive features were undoubtedly his light-grey eyes. They dominated his sunburned features and fascinated her, but something in his gaze was also slightly wounded and wary. It suggested that he didn't trust anyone easily. Zoe looked down at his hands holding his glass. He had long fingers, wide palms and neat nails.

'In brief, yes. My company is a traditional auction house, a family business; you won't find a better one. How long are you staying?'

'Until Friday. A friend is joining me tomorrow. We're planning to re-examine some shipping charts and dig out some more information. In the meantime, I'll check your company. I need to consider all the implications. As far as I know, I've never heard of anyone awarding exclusive auction rights before.'

Zoe moistened her lips and nodded. 'Perhaps such arrangements are never made public, or the treasure is always channelled into the hands of the same auctioneers because they had experience in that field,' she admitted honestly. 'There are auctioneers who specialise in this particular area.' She fumbled in her bag and put a visiting card down on the table. 'That's my telephone number, business and private.'

He picked it up and stuck it into his shirt pocket. He paused. 'I'll let you know.' He took a sip of coffee and started to ask Tony about mutual acquaintances, and they talked about shared events. Now and then, he checked his watch. Zoe didn't pay much attention to their conversation; she was still busy wondering if he'd accept or not.

'I have to go, Tony. I have an

invitation to dinner with some bigwig in an hour and need to go back to the hotel to change. I had to hire a black-tie outfit just for tonight.'

Zoe was busy imagining him James Bond-style, in a tuxedo, dress shirt and bow tie. He'd look just as craggy and sexy, and the image was thought-provoking. Her attention returned to the men as they got up. Alex addressed her specifically and remarked, 'Remember that if I do take up your offer, there's no quick turnaround. I stick to a contract and expect others to do the same. It might be months before you can expect results of any kind.' He got up.

She nodded. He was tall and slender and powerfully built. Zoe reckoned he'd stop at nothing once his mind was made up. He aimed to succeed and was prepared to take calculated risks. He was the type who often veiled his intelligence behind a thin screen of dry humour, although she hadn't noticed much of that just now. He was undoubtedly a very interesting man, the embodiment of a modern-day adventurer. Zoe preferred uncomplicated men who weren't too demanding; someone she could easily understand. Alex Harding didn't fit those categories. His explanations were calculated but . . . they were also honest and straightforward. He wouldn't be Tony's mate if he were a trickster.

'I'll be seeing you, Tony.' He gave her a brief nod.

Tony said, 'Yes, thanks for finding the time to see Zoe.'

He left them, threading his way through the tangle of chairs and tables towards the exit. He didn't look back as he pushed open the glass doors and flipped up the collar of his coat against the blustery wind.

She'd almost had to beg Tony to arrange this meeting. Tony knew him through his former girlfriend, Harding's cousin. As she watched Alex depart, she commented, 'I didn't reckon with him being English. Somehow, I imagined all treasure-hunters would be Americans.'

Tony shrugged a shoulder dismissively. 'I've never thought about it. Centuries ago English seamen chased treasure ships all over the known world, without any official blessings from above. We've all heard about a few famous English pirates, haven't we? What about Blackbeard? He came from Bristol.'

'This ship they'll be looking for was a man-of-war belonging to the English navy?'

He nodded. 'In those days it was sometimes a free-for-all on the high seas. Alex trained as a nautical engineer and worked for salvage companies for several years. This will be his second hunt. I don't know why he got involved in searching for sunken treasure. Perhaps he's descended from pirates, and blood will out. Perhaps he just wanted to opt out of the rat race for a while. I do know he's good at his job, has a first rate reputation, and takes everything he does seriously.'

'I expected him to be a controversial

character, but he seems quite serious and reliable.' Zoe relaxed. She knew she'd been extremely foolish to add her personal savings to those from the company. Thinking about it now, she wondered why she'd done so. Her company, Williams & Co., could afford to lose ten thousand, but she couldn't. She was usually very level-headed. Still . . . she'd given her word, and she'd stick to it.

Tony whistled softly. 'I didn't realize Williams & Co. was willing to invest so much. I wonder if Alex will accept.' He continued, 'Diving for sunken treasure is very risky. Do your bosses realize just how risky it is? I've heard about searches that led to nothing but bankruptcy for everyone involved.'

Zoe felt a weak film of perspiration on her upper lip. This definitely wasn't the moment to tell Tony that half of what she'd offered was her own money. Perhaps Alex Harding would simply turn down the offer and then nobody would ever know about her silliness.

She had the initial impression Alex Harding wasn't very interested, and he didn't need the money.

2

Next morning in the office, she reported back to her boss on the meeting. His bushy eyebrows shot halfway up his wrinkled forehead and he eyed her sceptically. 'My dear Zoe, salvaging shipping is not the same as salvaging sunken treasure. I still think it's a very chancy proposition. We're auctioneers, not the East India Company.'

Zoe pushed some loose hair off her face. 'George, we need new clients. We'll die out like the dodo if the company doesn't soon pull up its socks. We need to move with the times, catch public attention again, and encourage a new clientele.'

'If people read we're investing in a Caribbean treasure hunt, they're more likely to think we need our heads examined and run like lightening.'

'After listening to William's illusionary ideas at the last company meeting, I decided we had to do something. Fate intervened when Tony told me about Alex Harding's search. I checked him out on the internet. He's already conducted a successful search, off the Florida coastline. It didn't produce much booty but he found the wreck where he thought it might be. This time he's searching for a British ship that went down in the Caribbean in 1590. He's done the groundwork and even worked out a deal with the British government that will avoid years of litigation if he does actually find anything.'

'That doesn't mean it still isn't a high risk venture, or that he's not just another adventurer.'

'He'd have grabbed the money immediately if he was. It took some persuading to even get him to listen, and he still hasn't agreed yet. If he finds treasure, and we get the auctioning rights, the publicity would be tremendous. Sunken treasure would give us a shot in the arm and boost our reputation no end. By the way, thanks for persuading William to loosen the purse strings.'

He ran his hand over his thinning hair and grinned at her. 'It wasn't easy. Prising money out of William is a Herculean task. It wouldn't surprise me if he counts the number of sheets of toilet paper we use every day. One of these days he'll send everyone a memo telling us we have to bring our own. It's not surprising the company isn't doing well with someone like William in charge. He won't take risks; he's too conservative. He seems to think that when a client hears we're a company in the third generation, they'll simply fall over themselves to give us a commission.'

Zoe shifted in her seat and said nonchalantly, 'Did you know he plans to redecorate his office in a grand style, and that he's channelling some of our annual profits into a special account to pay for it?' Viewing George's somewhat dazed expression, she continued, 'In all probability he'll fork out money for a trendy interior decorator once he's amassed enough.'

His eyebrows lifted. 'No, I didn't. How do you know?'

'Rhonda from cashier's. She told me about it when she got smashed at our last Christmas party. I don't know if she remembered our conversation the next day. If she did, she certainly avoided mentioning it later. I expect she realizes if William knew she'd blabbed, he'd sack her for revealing confidential information. I persuaded Granville to check. He knows the appropriate passwords for the various classified accounts. He hinted, without quoting amounts, that if William parts with a couple of thousand from that account it definitely won't bankrupt the company.'

George scratched his chin. 'What a devious devil — I mean William, not Granville. He keeps telling me the company is tottering on its last legs, while he's squirreling away cash for brainless schemes!'

Zoe viewed him in satisfaction. 'Exactly! Even if he lost the money, William won't make a fuss. He'd need to explain to the board where the money came from in the first place, and they don't know about any secret accounts.'

George viewed her quizzically and blurted out, 'Zoe Michener! I didn't realize you spied. You've never had such hare-brained ideas before. Why now? Why this one?'

'Oh come on, George. If we don't do something radical soon it'll only be a matter of time until William starts throwing people out of their jobs. He puts the blame on everyone else, and never admits it's because of his mismanagement. I think it's remarkable that you've persuaded him to cough up. He's only hoping to swell the amount, of course. I thought that he'd be attracted by the idea of multiplying it fast, and I was right. He probably hasn't yet registered he could also lose every last penny if it goes wrong.'

He shrugged and then threw back his head to laugh. 'Zoe, you are incorrigible. It still sounds like an episode from a romantic Errol Flynn movie to me. Have you heard of Errol Flynn?'

'I've heard of him, but we have a modern counterpart these days called Johnny Depp. Getting back to this expedition . . . My friend Tony thinks it has a good chance of succeeding, mainly because Alex Harding is in charge.'

'And Tony is someone special? I thought you were going out with someone called Clive?'

She thought about faking the information and turning Tony into her latest boyfriend, because in this day and age it was a foregone conclusion that everyone met nice men all the time, and that you were a sought-after female. The truth was, it didn't happen like that at all. In fact, she'd never met anyone really special. She was beginning to think she never would.

She decided to be honest. George

was not only her boss; he was like an older brother. 'No, I finished with Clive weeks ago and I'm not looking for a replacement. I'm thoroughly disenchanted with men in general and happy to be single.'

'Tony is . . . ?'

'We went to school together. No romance; we're just very good friends. He's an ex-boyfriend of Alex Harding's cousin. That's how he knows Alex. They've kept in touch even though the romance fizzled out.'

His eyebrows lifted again and he picked up a pencil. 'What was his name again? God knows how the other directors will react if they find out William has secretly donated some money.' He checked the wall clock. 'I must be off. I'm auctioning at Walton Hall later this morning.'

Zoe rose and straightened her skirt. 'Have a good one.'

On the way out, she mused that he was right. Her idea was a little crazy, but perhaps it was worth a try.

3

Two days later Zoe and her best friend Lucy were having a girls' night. Lucy was manicuring her nails, watching the TV news, and listening to Zoe all at the same time. The two girls were lifelong friends and sometimes Zoe had the feeling they were even closer than sisters. Cooking them spaghetti with a rich tomato sauce, Zoe hoped Lucy wouldn't pay much attention when she mentioned meeting Alex Harding, why she'd met him, or how she'd added some of her own savings to boost her chances of success.

Lucy nearly knocked over a bottle of purple nail varnish from the arm of the cream settee. She shot up. 'Are you crazy? You've offered to put your savings into a crackpot treasure hunt?' Her dark eyes, with their heavy black mascara lashes, were huge round saucers.

Zoe swallowed hard. Lucy had been listening carefully after all. 'It's not a crackpot scheme. True, it's risky and a bit of a gamble, but it could work.'

'Where did you get such a mad idea?' Waving her hands around to speed up the drying process, Lucy waited impatiently for a reply.

Zoe saw Lucy's dyed red hair almost bristling with anger and she tried to calm her. 'Tony knows Alex Harding, and he mentioned he'd met him again recently. He told me what this chap was planning. I thought it was just the chance the company needs to catch public attention. I persuaded George to pump the money out of William, and somehow during the conversation I got carried away and topped the offer.'

With her eyes flashing, Lucy said, 'Are you crazy? Remember how long it took you to save that money? You kept telling me I ought to save, and not waste my money on clothes and shoes all the time.' She eyed her four-inch-high heels and their startling design. 'At least I have something to show for my money. You've thrown yours down the drain, and in the end you won't have anything from all your belt-tightening efforts.'

'William wasn't prepared to invest more than ten thousand, and this man didn't look interested, so . . . ' Zoe chewed her lip, looking troubled. 'Okay, I know what you mean. I was carried away by the idea and for some reason I wanted to be a part of it. If you'd met Alex Harding, you'd understand better. He isn't an opportunist. He impressed me. Our company needs a new impetus of some kind, or we'll all be queuing up at the job centre soon.'

Lucy's brows lifted and she smiled. 'Aha! So, in fact this all about the man! He must be very impressive for you to sacrifice your hard-earned money so easily.'

Zoe coloured and hastened to add, 'It has nothing to do with emotion. I was carried away by the idea, not by Alex Harding.'

Lucy tilted her head to the side. 'I know you. The man must have made an impact, but it doesn't explain why you're risking your personal savings. You'll get no extra thanks from your boss even if it succeeds. I hope to heaven this man refuses your offer.' She collected her various bits and pieces and tossed them into her capacious bag. 'I need something stronger than a cup of coffee. Is the pasta ready?' Zoe nodded. 'Good. Let's eat and then go down the pub. You can tell me all about the idea and about this man. I'll treat you to you a large vodka and lime. In fact, I need one very badly. That chap must have thought you were completely potty.'

Zoe put their food on the breakfast bar and they sat contentedly emptying their plates. Eventually she admitted, 'He doesn't realize it's not all company money. Somehow I think he would have turned it down straight away if he knew part of it came from me. Tony would've tried to stop me too.'

Lucy remarked, 'Quite rightly. Knowing how sensible you are, and how logically you act, it's incredible that you've done this in the first place.'

After finishing her pasta and piling their dishes on the draining board, Lucy hurried Zoe along. They grabbed their coats and Lucy tucked her arm through her friend's. 'Come on, let's go. As my granny used to say, there's no point in crying over spilt milk. Let's make the best of it.'

★   ★   ★

Alex Harding was due to leave tomorrow. Zoe checked the Swiss watch her parents gave her on her eighteenth birthday. Today had been a good one. She'd had a successful business meeting with a client this afternoon, and won a deal to auction off the contents of a family mansion in Sussex. Her flat was tidy and she didn't intend to stay in on the off chance that Alex would call. She'd phone Lucy instead and arrange to go to the pictures. She didn't want to think about the treasure hunt anymore. Perhaps it wasn't such a great idea after all.

Zoe tidied her hair and grabbed her bag. She was on her way to the door when the phone rang.

It was him. His deep voice stated, 'Zoe Michener? Zoe, I've thought about your offer . . . I've decided to accept.'

She took an audible deep breath. The inside of her mouth was dry but her voice was steady. 'Right, Mr Harding. That's good news.'

'I want to discuss the auction rights, and what that entails. It'd be helpful if we can meet again. Tomorrow perhaps? Or Wednesday morning?'

She hoped he didn't hear the nervousness in her voice. 'I thought you were leaving tomorrow?'

'I need a few extra days. I've arranged to study microfilms at the library tomorrow morning and have a meeting at five with someone from the Navy. Perhaps we can have lunch together? There's a neat little place down a side street near the National Maritime Museum.'

She was nervous. Her lack of experience with men like Alex Harding made her skittish and uncertain. She had no difficulty picturing his appealing features and broad shoulders, and that was a bad sign. He was in control, it was his treasure hunt, and he was a smart, sophisticated man into the bargain. 'That's near the *Cutty Sark*, isn't it? I presume my boss won't object if I take a longer lunch break if it's on company business. What time?' She felt breathless and was glad her composure was holding.

'I'll meet you on the steps of the Maritime Museum, main entrance, and for heaven's sake call me Alex not Mr Harding.'

She didn't comment. 'On the steps at — ?'

'Twelve-thirty? I've already had our lawyers fax me an agreement on your percentage gain and auction rights, if we're successful. You can take a quick look tomorrow and tell me if you agree.'

'I'm sure you won't object if I give it to our company lawyer to check. You'll get it back fast, promise.'

Zoe thought she heard a faint chuckle. 'Fine by me. Till tomorrow then. Bye!'

There was a click. Zoe was glad of the anonymity; she felt how extra colour covered her neck and cheeks. She needed to steel herself and prepare for the situation before she met him again tomorrow. How? Usually meeting strange men didn't bother her; it was part of her job. But Alex Harding was different.

4

During their meeting at the restaurant, when she played with her food and drank a glass of wine without enjoyment, he suddenly shocked her. 'I've decided you ought to check your investment on the spot, so you know where your money is going and have no cause to complain later.'

'What do you mean, on the spot? In the Caribbean?'

He nodded, and she felt extremely flustered. 'You mean someone from my company? I presume you mean my boss.'

'No, I mean you. You instigated everything and you should approve or disapprove.'

Trying not to bluster, she said, 'I don't know a thing about boats, searches, the Caribbean, or sunken treasure. It'd be a waste of time. Anyway, my boss won't give me time off, and what about the airfare? Our director counts the pennies, and he'll consider it an unnecessary expense.'

'My friend couldn't join me. That's why I'm still here and will be for few more days. You can use his ticket. It's an open one because we were never sure if he could make it. I've already cleared things with your boss. I spoke to a Mr William Williams this morning and explained what I wanted. He said it was perfectly okay as long as there was no extra expense involved.'

The breath seemed to leave her lungs. She looked away then back at him and said quietly, 'I wish you'd asked me beforehand. It seems I have no say in the matter, doesn't it? When are you planning to leave?' She felt she'd been run over by a steamroller, and she was beginning to object to his overhand attitude, even if he was a very attractive man.

A short time later she left him heading back to his researches, and she sauntered towards the next underground station. She recalled how he looked as he sat opposite her. He was refined and classy, and she followed his clever conversation about his job and future intentions with interest. It was a pleasant meal until the moment he dropped the bombshell. Why did he think someone had to check him, the boat, or anything else? He'd already said he didn't like interfering busybodies evaluating him or what he did. She never reckoned with this. He was deliberately involving her and she didn't understand why.

Back at work, Zoe explained with heightened colour to their company lawyer that she'd added some personal money to that of the company because she believed it was a great chance to earn some extra cash. She asked him to formulate the agreement in such a way that the amount stated was split between the company and her, without it being too obvious. He raised his eyebrows and reminded her about the risk she was taking before he wrapped it up in legal phraseology. Even Zoe had to think twice about the actual meaning when she read through the contract because he referred initially to her as responsible for settling the deal, and later discreetly formulated her to be one of two parties who were actually financing the amount. She sent it around to Alex's hotel and if he noticed the subtle turn of the wording, he didn't say so. He signed the company's copy and sent it back. Zoe spent a frantic two days getting her work up to date and thinking about whether she had suitable clothes for sunnier climes.

Lucy came around on the evening before she left, armed with some dazzling items that Zoe would never wear. In April the shops weren't exactly plastered with summer wear, but Zoe wouldn't have been able to go shopping anyway, as she was too busy with other things. Lucy had a heyday discarding Zoe's choices and packing a holdall with her own replacements. After Lucy left, Zoe repacked the bag with her less flamboyant selection of last year's fashions. She would never wear Lucy's skimpy, sultry kind of clothes, but didn't have the heart to tell her so.

Next morning she left for the airport, still dazed by the speed of happenings. Three hours later, Zoe Michener was in an aeroplane sitting next to Alex Harding, on her way to the Caribbean.

5

She preceded him down the aisle, trying to avoid the other harassed passengers still loading their possessions in the overhead lockers. He gestured her towards the window seat. Apart from the usual kind of hackneyed phrases between two people who were almost strangers, they hadn't spoken very much to each other since they'd met outside departures.

She fixed her safety belt and felt nervous. She'd neglected to ask him where their final destination in the Caribbean was, and presumed he'd provide the information. He didn't, and now she was waiting for an opportunity to ask.

After take-off and the obligatory orange juice and nuts, she asked, 'I expect you've done this trip very often.'

He was busy pulling a bundle of

papers out of his bag. He didn't look up and sounded offhand and unresponsive. 'Too often.'

He immediately set about studying his papers, and she took the hint. She supposed that it was usual for his high-handed attitude. Why on earth should he chatter and satisfy the curiosity of someone like her, unless she asked something? On the other hand, they hardly knew each other, and as he'd organized the flight, it could just be thoughtlessness on his part. She rummaged in her bag for a paperback but wasn't focused. She jammed the small cushion into place next to the window and tried to find a comfortable position.

She must have catnapped. The sound of the meal trolley woke her and she was embarrassed to find that her head had fallen onto Alex's shoulder. She coloured and straightened. 'Sorry!' He was still busy with his papers. They must be terribly important.

She didn't notice how his mouth had

an upward turn. 'No problem. I'd have pitched you elsewhere if it bothered me.' Nodding towards the approaching stewardess, he added, 'I told them you'd take the chicken.'

She nodded and massaged her neck, glad to fill in some time with the meal. She looked out of the window, pretending she could spot something interesting, and then at her book again. Alex was a reserved man and normally Zoe preferred someone like that to a loud, talkative one. But for some reason, this time his polite disregard irritated her. Time passed and soon she glimpsed occasional islands far below, so she presumed they were already crossing the Caribbean. Secretly she wished she were going on holiday instead of heading for an unknown destination with Alex Harding. She'd never been to this part of the world before.

After landing, they passed through friendly passport controls and zigzagged their way through the other jostling passengers. Zoe wasn't happy to trot after Alex like his pet dog, but she had no choice. She reluctantly admitted that it was pleasant to let someone else organize everything. It gave her time to absorb her surroundings. Once they were outside arrivals, he signalled for a taxi.

At last, she asked, 'Where are we going?'

Looking surprised and suddenly conscious of his shortcoming, he uttered, 'Sorry! I forgot to tell you, didn't I? We catch a plane from here to St. Thomas. I hope Billy will be there to meet us, with the boat for the last stage.'

'And our final destination is . . . ?'

'A small island called Jost van Dyke. It's only a harbouring point for us at the moment. Our main base is normally Jamaica. That's where we put the whole search together, and bought most of the equipment.' He watched her and wondered how many women he knew who would have spent hours flying to an unknown destination without bombarding him with continual chatter. She was unusual.

She nodded. At least she now knew

where they were going. He seemed to take everything, including her, for granted. The smell of the island was a mixture of sweet-scented blossoms, aromatic shrubs and the salty ocean. It flowed round her face and ruffled her hair. It was fantastic. The temperatures were still comfortably warm even if the peak season was over. Somehow, the fact that she was with a strange man in the Caribbean was very unreal.

When they finally met Billy, the excitement of travelling to an exotic destination was beginning to wear off. They'd been travelling most of the day.

Alex introduced her. 'This is Zoe Michener, from the auction house in London.'

He nodded and Alex explained, 'Billy is my right-hand man.'

Zoe made an effort to be friendly to the sunburned middle-aged American as he helped her aboard the swaying ship. Before they set off, Billy offered her some welcome cold juice and then he and Alex made their way to the bridge.

She trailed after them and sat down in a corner. She gathered that the rest of the crew were on Jost van Dyke. Although the speed they went over the surface of the water was fast and bumpy, it was still wonderful to be skimming across turquoise waters in a tropical world. They anchored offshore and used the ship's small dinghy with its outboard motor to reach the beach. Even then, she found that they had to wade the last meters.

Billy explained, 'The only pier is on the other side of the island, and I thought it'd be easier for you to go ashore here than to have to walk the coastal road after your long journey. I've booked you into a local campground. It's clean and cheap.'

'Thanks, Billy!' She was glad she was wearing cotton jeans and not a skirt that would most likely balloon around her in the water. Alex leapt fluidly overboard, took her holdall and waded towards the white sandy beach holding it above his head. She slipped overboard to follow him through the clear water. It felt enticingly warm as it flowed across her thighs. All she wanted now was a shower, a rest and some time on her own.

Billy had already turned the dinghy to head towards the ship. Looking back, she noted for the first time that Alex's ship was quite sizeable. She followed him up the road and wished she'd grabbed her holdall from him. She didn't like being beholden to Alex Harding for anything. They reached an arched entrance covered in climbing bougainvillea, and went through the swinging doors into an untidy office. A ventilator circled sluggishly above them. Alex shouted, and a woman with a generous figure and chocolate skin appeared from out back. Judging by the feeling of familiarity and exchange of greetings, the woman knew Alex well. She gave him a broad smile and handed Zoe a key.

Pushing his peaked cap off his head, he turned to her. 'I'll pick you up in a couple of hours. We'll go to a local eating place and then you can meet the rest of the crew.'

'You don't stay here?'

'No. We all live on board, but don't worry, Florence will take care of you.'

Zoe nodded and eyed the dark-skinned woman behind the desk, who smiled at her. 'Fine.' She picked up her holdall and looked at the number attached to the key.

Florence said, 'I'll show you to your cabin.'

Alex asked, 'Need help with the luggage?'

'No thanks!' She followed Florence outside.

Alex watched her walk away and admired the way her jeans clung to her form and her rounded bottom. Her thighs were still wet from the seawater.

★   ★   ★

Zoe glimpsed the ocean through the palms on the way to the cabin. The colours and view were breathtaking.

When Florence reached the chosen cabin, Zoe found it was bare-bones, and basic in appearance. The toilets and showers were among the palm and tamarind trees facing the sea. Everything was clean and tidy and she sighed in contentment.

Florence asked, 'Are you another of Alex's girlfriends?'

She shook her head. 'No, just a business acquaintance. Does he have a lot of girlfriends?'

Florence chuckled. 'He seems to change them more often than some men change their underwear. Have a good night's sleep. I'll bring your breakfast tomorrow. What time?'

'Thanks. Is eight-thirty okay?'

'Fine.'

Florence left her alone with the sounds of the sea. She was tired and glad she had time to relax before she met the rest of the crew. She stripped to her underwear and slipped gratefully between the cool cotton sheets. In a matter of minutes, the never-ending sound of the waves hitting the beach just a few meters away helped to lull her into a dreamless sleep.

6

The sound of a door banging nearby woke her. The sunlight had faded and it was cooler. An invigorating shower, and a light top and cotton skirt, went a long way to restoring her wellbeing. She'd packed pretty items that were a lot more sensible than Lucy's choice of flamboyant and daring clothes.

She checked the time and walked to the office. Alex was already waiting; he was chatting and making Florence laugh. He clearly knew how to charm, though he'd never given Zoe any special attention, and she didn't know what to think about that. Perhaps he thought she was too professional and competent; too business-like and not feminine enough. The idea poked uneasily at the back of her brain, but she couldn't pretend to be what she wasn't. She shrugged and joined them.

Scrutinizing him, she understood why women found him deliciously appealing even if she didn't. She felt a prickle along her spine as she considered his looks. He had an air of authority about him and a lazy seductiveness in those light eyes. She also noticed how he eyed her outfit and seemed to approve. She relaxed.

'Ready?'

'Yes. What about my passport, money, etcetera? Can I leave them here?'

'Give them to Florence. She'll lock them in the safe.'

She fumbled in her bag, kept some cash, and gave the rest to Florence. Zoe also managed a polite smile when he held the swing-door open. Walking leisurely by his side, she decided to ask more questions. 'Why start from here? Is this island especially suitable?'

'It's closer to the search area, and we needed somewhere to make the final checks before we set off. I also happen to like it here.'

They walked along a narrow sidewalk towards a brightly lit building at the end of the street. Music wafted towards them. Most of the shack-like buildings along the street were in darkness. The balmy breezes fondled her face and felt wonderful.

They reached the open doorway of the eating place and he guided her towards a table on the far side of the room. Pop-sounding reggae music warbled from the stereo speakers squeezed between rows of dusty bottles on the shelf. The room was full, and conversation and laughter flowed between the scantily clad customers. Diffuse yellow light shone onto the tables, but most of the room was smothered in shadows and drifts of cigarette smoke. The man behind the bar shouted a raucous greeting to Alex.

Alex grinned at him and lifted two fingers. Soon after, a tired-looking waitress brought them two glasses of cold beer. Zoe had rarely enjoyed anything more. She gulped at it gratefully, and as the cold liquid slipped down her throat she looked at Alex and said, 'I could drink a barrelful.'

He looked amused. 'Go ahead! But leave room for a pain killer.'

'A pain killer? What, a headache tablet?'

He laughed and it changed his expression entirely. 'No. It's a famous cocktail. Everyone who comes here drinks it. I'll order one for you with the meal.'

'Sounds good.' She hoped it wasn't too potent. She studied the few lines of hand-written items on the dog-eared one-page-menu. 'When are you planning to leave?'

'As soon as we've sorted out the last hiccups. Perhaps in a day or two. Billy will be here soon, with the others.'

She nodded and looked around, enjoying the atmosphere. She also didn't want to admit she enjoyed being with someone who plainly attracted the attention of other females.

A voluptuous girl with long black hair and flashing eyes hurried to their table and threw herself onto Alex's lap. His chair creaked and moved dangerously under the added weight. She laughed and wrapped her arms round his shoulders and gave him a kiss on his cheek. His hand slid automatically around her waist, and a broad smile spread across his face as he eyed her in appreciation. 'Hi, Maria! How are things? Have you missed me?'

'You? Why would I miss you?'

'So you haven't?' One eyebrow lifted quizzically and he grinned. With one arm holding the girl tightly, he faced Zoe.

'Maria, I want you to meet Zoe. Her company has contributed money to our search. I thought it was a good idea for her to see the boat and meet everyone. Zoe, this is Maria Sanchez, a friend and a first-class operator of various bits of machinery on board.'

Maria focussed her attention on Zoe, summing her up in one sweep of her coal-black eyes. Alex made no attempt to shift her from his lap. She tossed back the mass of black wavy hair and spoke to him in Spanish. It cut Zoe neatly out of the conversation.

For a few seconds Zoe felt angry, until she pulled herself together and reminded herself that this was none of her business; his private life was his concern. She didn't need to understand Spanish to realize that she was the focus of their conversation. Maria stared at her with questioning eyes. Alex's reply in Spanish sounded fluent. In English, he explained. 'Maria comes from San Diego. I've known her for ages.' He pushed her gently off his lap and indicated the adjoining chair. Without any protest, Maria slipped into it. She looked irritated, and Zoe wondered if it was because of herself. She needn't have worried; Maria could have Alex Harding on a silver plate as far as she was concerned.

Maria said, 'Billy and the others are on the way.'

Zoe pushed her hair behind her ears and viewed them. If Alex and this girl were a twosome, she'd calm Maria's misgivings. 'I expect you have a lot to talk about. I'll eat and leave you to catch up on the news. I can talk to the others another time. I don't want to butt in.'

Alex leaned forward to challenge her composure with his disturbing light eyes. 'You couldn't muscle in on us even if you tried, could she, Maria?'

She wasn't quite sure what he meant but clearly, he and Maria seemed intimate friends. Maria giggled and Zoe shrugged. 'It was only an offer,' Zoe said. She emptied her glass in a single gulp and was glad to hold something. The colour burned in her cheeks. Alex eyed her silently, and then the waitress appeared again to take their order. He ordered food and three new beers.

Zoe was annoyed and baffled because she wanted to ignore him, and couldn't. She concentrated on reflecting that after the crew left she'd still have time to enjoy the island. It looked like paradise. What bonded Alex and Maria together was none of her business.

The food arrived just as a group of men bustled in and joined them. Alex beckoned them across and they dragged extra chairs around the table. They were evidently interested in Zoe and waited patiently for Alex to make the introductions. They were outdoor men with tanned skins, muscled bodies and calloused hands. She'd already met the oldest one, Billy. He was proclaimed to be Alex's right-hand man. His blue eyes twinkled, and deep lines crossed his tanned face. Zoe smiled at them all as Alex named them, and felt her tension lessening.

Billy ran his hand over his face. 'How's the accommodation?'

'I love it,' Zoe said. 'I think I'm the only guest.'

'Yeah, well, the peak season has gone. People still come though. You won't be on your own for long, I'm sure.' Billy turned to his neighbour. 'Hank's wife has stayed here and she liked it. Hank comes from Dallas.'

Hank said, 'Howdy! You sure have a cute accent.'

'Do I?' Zoe laughed. 'Your accent is cute too.'

He chuckled. 'I guess so!'

The other man, Gary — a mountain of a man in a checked shirt — gave her a toothy smile and an encouraging look. 'I'm responsible for the mechanical side of things.' He nodded across the table. 'Maria is our expert on air supplies and anything to do with that. Hank turns his hand to whatever's needed, Billy drives us all mad with his safety rules, and Alex tries, unsuccessfully, to lord it over the rest of us.'

They all laughed and Zoe's heart skipped a beat when she saw how often Alex smiled and joked with them. It revealed another side to his character. He nodded complacently at their comments and jibes. The warmth of his smile was obvious when he joined in. She almost wished she belonged to their camaraderie. They seemed to all get on famously, and that was probably essential for a successful hunt. She couldn't help but notice how Maria eyed Alex frequently, and how she chatted quietly to him over her glass of beer.

During the meal — chicken again, in a delicious coconut sauce — the men told Zoe about what they'd done before joining Alex. Maria had helped her father, who was a deep-sea diver. All the others came from salvaging companies, and were happy to be part of an expedition that wasn't taking place in the cold Atlantic or some other dangerous spot of the world's oceans. The atmosphere improved and relaxed as the men got used to her.

Alex said, 'We'll show you round the boat tomorrow.'

She nodded. 'Yes, I'll be interested.' She tried to show that she'd tried to grasp what they were doing. 'I read that it's difficult to actually pinpoint a wreck, even if people think they know where it went down. Time, currents, storms, false eyewitness reports, misleading rocks on the ocean floor, those things make searching difficult, don't they? It sounds like looking for a needle in a haystack.'

Excitedly, Billy said, 'Yes, there are some real big companies sifting the seabed for treasure these days. We're small fry in comparison, but they can't cover every inch of the planet, and they have huge overheads to keep fleets of ships and expensive systems busy all the time. That gives smaller teams like ours the chance to out-manoeuvre them, because our overheads are negligible in comparison.'

Zoe already liked Billy. She thought the other men seemed nice too, but there was something particularly endearing about him. She listened to them talking about where they came from, and about their friends. Hank talked about his wife and little girl.

'Doesn't your wife mind, Hank?' Zoe asked him.

He ordered another beer. 'No! Dolly's used to it. I've worked on salvage rigs for years and she's used to waiting for me. She keeps herself busy by running a bookshop. Now that we have a little girl, she has less time than ever to miss me. She knows how the sea is in my blood and accepts that as part of me.'

Zoe wondered if she'd be content with seeing a husband every couple of weeks or months. Maria was fairly quiet, and Zoe wished she could reassure her that she was only here to look at the boat and leave. She didn't want to do so in front of Alex in case he made a sarcastic remark. After a while she pushed her plate away. 'That was good.' She looked around briefly and got up. Her chair scraped the floor noisily. 'I enjoyed the meal and meeting you all. Goodnight, I'll see you tomorrow.' She picked up her shoulder bag and slung it over her shoulder. On the way to the open doorway, she found that Alex was following her.

He uttered, 'I'll see you back to the hotel.'

'Don't bother; it's not necessary. I can manage on my own.'

His pale eyes were piercing. 'I think you enjoy being at loggerheads with me, don't you?' He gestured. 'Lead the way!'

She gave in. The raucous sounds of laughter and snatches of the foot-tapping music followed them for a while until they faded completely. They strolled along the sidewalk in silence and Zoe's sandals slapped on the wooden surface as they went.

There was no one about and she was deep in thought when someone dashed out of a side street, bumping into her. It was so unexpected, she automatically grabbed at anything to steady herself. It happened to be Alex, and he held on to her. Locked in his arms, and only inches from each other, their eyes met in the darkness. The shadows dimmed his face but his eyes still gleamed with an unspoken message. He eased his hold but her arms were still cradled against his chest. For a moment, everything hung suspended and she wished she could breathe normally. She felt the hardness of his body and inhaled his spicy fragrance mixed with the salt of the sea. His smile emerged for a few seconds and he made her feel like a sixteen-year-old. It was a thrill mixed with anticipation of the unknown.

Zoe pulled away and heard some mumbled words of apology from someone hurrying off in the opposite direction. She stared after him and straightened before she cleared her throat and said, 'Thanks!'

His voice was deep and evocative. 'You're welcome. Perhaps you're glad I came after all?'

She admitted reluctantly, 'Perhaps!' She set off again and he fell into step alongside, both concentrating on reaching the campground without any more mishaps. When they arrived she was almost relieved. There was something about Alex that spelt danger. He wasn't her type of man, and she had a feeling she wasn't able to handle him. She turned and asked, 'What time do you want me to come tomorrow?'

'Whenever you like. You know where it is?'

'Roughly. Billy explained it's on the other side of the island.'

'Yes. This is a very small island. If you follow the coastal road, you'll reach us in a matter of minutes.'

'Billy mentioned a pier?'

'Yes, it is the only place we can lift something heavy on or off the ship. That's not possible elsewhere; the waters are too shallow. Our boat is the largest one there at the moment. You can't miss it. You've already been on the *Astrea*.'

'Why did you call it 'Astrea'? The name of a girlfriend?'

'No, it was the name of the Roman galley ship in *Ben-Hur*.'

She didn't comment. She'd never met a man quite like him. In some ways he was like any other, but there was something about him that stimulated her imagination in a special way. She wished he didn't; it meant she wasn't completely in control.

'Thanks! Goodnight!' she said.

'Goodnight! Sleep well!'

Zoe wondered if she could. She left him standing and went down to the deserted beach for a few minutes. She stared at the undulating water and the reflection of the silver moon floating on the surface.

Back in her cabin-like hut, she found she wasn't really tired. This was a foreign world and she was dealing with things and people she knew nothing about. She made herself comfortable and began to read, and the story finally caught her imagination. She thought about Alex and Maria too. They seemed closer than just a boss and worker. Maria was welcome to him! She thumped the pillows and made a comfortable hollow. He was organizing a hunt for treasure; anything else was irrelevant. She'd try to enjoy the short visit, and not let him or Maria steal all the pleasure.

7

Zoe didn't fall asleep until the early hours of the morning, but woke again when the first rays of the sun began to paint the world outside in silent shades of gold and orange. Leaning out of the window, she watched in awe for a while, then dressed quickly in jeans and a white blouse and went for a walk around the bay with its enticing smells, waving palms and straggly rocks. She was alone there and it was a special feeling. On her return, Florence was waiting with her breakfast. She'd laid it on a table outside her cabin. The friendly owner lingered and told her a little about the island. After she'd finished, Zoe decided it was time to do her duty and take a closer look at Alex Harding's boat.

It was still early morning when she strolled along the main road that curved around the edge of the island.

On one side was the glittering sea, and on the other a mixture of palms, cacti and trees smothered in something that looked like orange spaghetti. The island was hilly and she met no one, except one man pulling a cart in the direction of the campground.

In a matter of minutes she reached an inlet with an apology for a pier. Some other yachts were bobbing on the turquoise waters, but the *Astrea* was moored next to the pier. It seemed bigger than it had yesterday, but perhaps she'd been too tired to register things properly. It looked in first-class condition. The paintwork was pristine, the gangplank clean, the ropework stowed neatly away, and no technical bits and pieces muddling empty spaces. Uncertain of whether to go on board without invitation, she watched the boat as it bobbed up and down for a moment, until Billy spotted her.

He welcomed her with a smile on his weathered face. 'Morning, Zoe! Coming on board?'

She smiled back. 'Yes. I hope I won't get in your way. The only boats I've ever been on before are the ferries between Britain and France, so this is quite a contrast.'

He laughed gruffly. 'This is a decent size for the job it's meant to do. That's why it's flatter in shape too, making it easier for loading and unloading, and fixing a diving platform. There's a lot of technical stuff for searching and recovery on board so there isn't a lot of living space, but sailors are used to cramped conditions.' He held out his hand. 'Take off your shoes, you'll find it's a lot easier to walk around.'

Zoe took off her sandals and reached for his hand. Once on board, it didn't take long to adjust. It really was enjoyable to walk barefoot on the warm wooden planking.

'Follow me!'

She did. Hank and Gary were busy working on something that Billy explained was a blower. They shouted hello and waved when they saw her. Maria had a clipboard in her hands and was checking supplies. She looked up. Her brow wrinkled. Zoe buried her own caginess and said pleasantly, 'Hi, Maria.'

'Hi!'

Billy urged her on. 'Alex is in the wheelhouse. You'd better say hello!'

Glancing beyond the railing, back towards a nearby beach, Zoe felt sheer delight when she viewed the spotless white sand and palm trees merging with the gentle turquoise water. The sun was high in a cloudless blue sky and there was a smell of the salty sea. She'd be free to do as she wished after the ship left. It'd be heaven to just laze around! Once she'd finished here, she'd return to the hotel and have a catnap. It was already warm and she'd been up since dawn.

She followed Billy up the steps into the small wheelhouse with its panorama windows. Alex was bent over a high desk on the side, studying a chart. The sunshine from an adjacent windowpane made his sun-bleached hair look even blonder. The sight of him produced an unexpected, pleasant feeling inside. He rolled up the map, pushed it into a tube and patted it before he looked up. Zoe's throat felt dry. Perhaps it had something to do with the fact that he was an Englishman and they were in a foreign environment.

He gave her an imperceptible nod and asked, 'And? Is it worth your company's investment?'

'It looks great to me, although I don't have a clue about boats or any of the equipment, so that's probably a worthless comment. If you don't find treasure, no one will ever ask about the state of the ship. Only success or failure will be remembered.' She hastened to soften her comments. 'It was kind of you to invite me to take a look around, but someone else from the company with more nautical knowledge might have been a more sensible choice. I'm a nautical zilch.'

Billy chuckled and remarked, 'She's never been on a small boat before this one. She just told me the smallest thing she's ever been before on was one of those big passenger ferries.'

Alex's eyes twinkled and the corner of his mouth twitched. 'Then welcome to the world of real sailors. If we had time, I'd take you out on a trial run to see how you like riding the waves, but we're almost ready to leave. I've arranged to meet someone tomorrow. He's got a water dredger I'd like to buy.' Without knowing what that was and not wanting to show her ignorance, she just nodded. 'Once the crew has finished today's work, we'll be off.'

Zoe looked around. 'Good! I won't interrupt you any more then.'

'Show her the cabins and the galley, Billy. I'm sure she'll be more interested in them than our sonar devices or any of this gear.' Alex picked up a sailor's peaked cap and gestured. 'Feel free to look around. Billy will be glad to answer any questions.'

It was clear he didn't intend to waste time on showing her around, but if they were planning to leave today, he possibly had plenty to do. 'Thanks. If I don't see you again, good luck! I would like to hear how things are going, if you have time. Just a short email would be great. It will stop my boss harassing me and asking if I've heard anything or what you're doing.'

He viewed her without answering before he turned away and left the cabin. Billy explained some of the equipment in the wheelhouse and then she followed him below deck.

'As you see, Alex is a stickler for keeping things shipshape, and I agree with him. You can't afford clutter on a boat this size. It leads to accidents and mishaps. Tidy surroundings also make everyone feel better.'

She nodded. 'If you only have limited space, you need to be tidy.'

He showed her the cramped quarters with a tier of three bunk beds for the three crewmen, then Maria's small cabin and finally Alex's slightly bigger cabin. As expected, it was also very spick and span. It was a man's room, in simple lines and toned colours, although there were a couple of personal touches. There were some photos on the wall and a shelf full of books arranged behind a protective rail.

Billy asked, 'Thirsty?'

She smiled. 'Yes, I am. I haven't got used to the different temperatures yet. I think I'm dehydrated.'

'Right. I'll get you something before you leave. Sit down and make yourself comfortable. I'll be right back with a nice cool drink.'

He bustled off and Zoe sat down in a large leather chair with side wings. It faced the neatly made bunk bed opposite. She felt drowsy and closed her eyes. She woke again seconds later, startled by the sound of voices, and she willed herself to stay awake but enjoyed closing her eyes and just trying to listen. The sounds on board faded and the waves hitting the hull sent her back to sleep again.

When she woke, she had a stiff neck.

Slightly confused, she adjusted to her surroundings again, and wondered where Billy was. She looked at her watch. That couldn't be right! She'd been in the cabin over three hours! She jumped to her feet and grabbed the back of the chair. She heard the regular throbbing of the ship's motor. They were moving! Holding on, she struggled towards the door, down the short corridor, and up the steps. She saw greenish-blue water all around. Where was the pier? Where was the land?

Footsteps padded round the corner and stopped in mid-passage. Audibly, Alex drew in his breath. 'What the hell are you doing here?'

8

She stared at him. Her own expression was equally shocked. 'I . . . I don't know! I was in your cabin. Billy went to get me something to drink. I sat down and I fell asleep.'

'Billy told me you'd left.'

'Why did he say that? I wouldn't have gone without saying goodbye to everyone. He didn't come back to your cabin; he would have found me.'

'He did. I saw him on his way back with a can of coke.' He paused. 'Wait a minute. Were you sitting in my winged chair?'

She nodded.

'That explains it. He came back, glanced in, didn't see you, and thought you'd left.' He ran his hand through his thick hair. 'What the hell am I going to do now?'

'I'm sorry. How far are we from land?

You'll have to take me back.'

He considered her for a moment. Was it just her imagination, or was his serious expression tinged with something else — something more intriguing? 'That's out of the question! I told you earlier that I've arranged to meet up with a mate of mine in the hope he'll sell me a piece of equipment. We arranged to meet at sea, because he's on his way to Antigua. I haven't got time to taxi you back.'

'Surely you can do a quick turnabout to deposit me on land somewhere?' She knew it was her own fault, but why couldn't he be more helpful?

'No I can't.' His voice was brusque. 'If you fall asleep where Billy couldn't see you, you'll have to live with the consequences. I won't make it to our agreed meeting point if I turn back now.'

'But you'll take me back after you've met his man?'

He paused for a moment and his mouth turned up at the corner. She didn't like the amusement in his face when he shrugged his shoulders and said in a casual tone, 'Sorry! I planned to head directly to the search area from there.'

She spluttered, 'But you can't. I have to fly home at the weekend. I can't stay on board.'

He looked towards the railing. 'I suppose you could make it on your own, if you're a really good swimmer, but keep a watch out for the occasional shark on the way.' He half-turned away, trying to hide his enjoyment on noticing how he'd disrupted her cool. He cleared his throat. 'I don't propose to change my plans.'

Her concern was gradually replaced by anger and she tried to keep her temper and face him. She pushed her hair off her face and persevered. 'And what about my job in London? You were the one who insisted on me coming, although I warned you that someone else was better suited. I didn't mean to fall asleep; you know that. You could help, if you were more considerate.' She looked around with a fraught expression. Amusement flickered in his eyes, but he didn't comment.

Zoe said, 'Are you near another island, or passing one on the way? You could put me ashore and then I'd find my own way back to the hotel from there.'

'How will you manage that without any money, and no passport? I could lend you some money, I suppose, but a lot of these islands belong to different nationalities. You need your passport to move anywhere.'

She tried not to let anger triumph over rationality. 'You can't do this! You can't just take me with you. It's kidnapping!'

'Believe me, I don't want you here, but that's how it is. Your presence causes me a lot of extra problems, so stop bellyaching. Until I've had time to sort things out, stay out of everyone's way, don't touch anything, sit down somewhere, and keep quiet. I need to talk things through with Billy and find out what the others think — but I don't have time to do that at present. Perhaps we can sort something out after we've met up with my friend.' He turned away, still mumbling. If Zoe had seen his expression, it would have only increased her antagonism and resentment. His eyes were twinkling and a smile plastered his face.

Zoe formed her hands into tight fists. The man was impossible. She hated him. She sat down on a nearby metal drum and held on to a tightly anchored cable. In a short time, she suddenly realized the movement of the ship was making her feel sick. Her stomach was sending out warning signals and she wished she could control it.

★　★　★

Alex came into the cabin. She felt terrible. 'Please go away and let me die in peace,' she moaned.

He laughed and left the cabin door

open to admit fresh air, and replace the smell of sickness. 'Billy told me you aren't feeling too good. If you came outside and focused your sight on the horizon, it might help.' He almost sounded sympathetic. 'I've brought you some more drinking water and a glass of boiled water with ginger. Billy says it works a treat for some people.'

He was despicable. It was entirely his fault. The nausea took over in waves once more, and she sat up quickly. That only made her even dizzier but she forced her legs over the bunk and willed herself to ignore the vertigo and the oncoming sickness while she dashed to the bathroom. She barely made it. On her knees in front of the toilet, she felt as weak as a kitten. He picked up a facecloth and bent over her to wipe her face. For a few seconds the cooling effect of the damp cotton helped her. He threw the facecloth into the washbasin, and hoisted her to her feet. He slid his arm around her waist as they struggled sideways like two drunken crabs through the narrow doorway back into the cabin. Glancing at a wall mirror, she saw she had a face as white as ghost and her baggy body looked just as unattractive in her grubby blouse and crumpled jeans. She looked frightful. In fact, she'd never looked worse. She tumbled gratefully on to the bed and tried to hang on to the last shreds of her dignity. 'I'm sorry! I must smell dreadful.'

He grinned. 'Not exactly like a bed of roses, but don't worry, I've experienced worse.'

Holding her head in her hands, she sounded as despondent as she felt. 'If you'd taken me back, this wouldn't have happened.' She tried to save her pride and said, 'I wouldn't have made such a fool of myself and caused all this extra trouble.'

He shrugged. 'You might be surprised to know that sometimes even weathered sailors get seasick. I read it has something to do with how your brain copes with two conflicting messages. You feel the up and down motion, and your brain cells have trouble matching it to what's actually happening. Even I was seasick once, in the middle of an almighty storm in the middle of the Atlantic, so don't worry about it. Apparently, stress or bad experience sometimes causes seasickness too. Some people are scared of heights, others are frightened of spiders, and some get seasick.'

She groaned. 'Don't make me think about heights, or ups and down, please! Just the sound of those words gives me the collywobbles.'

He squatted down in front of her. The remarkable light grey eyes were kind and sympathetic for a change. 'I really think it'll help if you sit in the fresh air and focus your sight on the horizon. You need to concentrate on one spot and not let your glance wander around.' He tilted his head to the side and his eyes twinkled. 'I'll provide you with a bucket, so you won't have to heave overboard!'

Sounding resentful, she said, 'I'll

never get on a boat like this again as long as I live.'

He laughed. 'You managed the trip to Jost van Dyke without any trouble, so you don't automatically get seasick.'

'The sea wasn't as choppy when we made that trip.'

Holding out his hand, he continued, 'Come on, give it a try. It might divert your thoughts for a while. Lying there looking up at the ceiling and waiting for the next wave of nausea won't help. Usually the Caribbean is very calm at this time of the year. Granted, it is choppier than usual this afternoon, but I can assure you it's nothing compared to stormy weather in the rainy season.'

She knew she needed to show him some kind of gratitude. He'd stood by watching her being sick. He must have a stomach like a mule. She'd make an effort and try what he suggested. She thanked the gods that she hadn't yet been sick over his bunk or anything else in his cabin. Silently, she accepted his supporting hand around her waist and they left the stuffy cabin. They tottered along the narrow gangway and upstairs to the main deck. He took her to a nearby metal storage chest that was partly sheltered from the gusty winds, then disentangled his hold. Zoe leaned back and closed her eyes. Even though she still felt weak and extremely stupid, the fresh air was good. She opened them again and concentrated on a spot on the horizon. It was dead centre between two of the ship's rigging lines.

Alex disappeared and came back with the mug of boiled ginger, some bottled water and a bucket that he swilled out with seawater before he put it down next to her. 'Try a sip of the boiled stuff now and then, if you can. Drink plenty of water too. Maybe you were already dehydrated when you came on board, and now your body has lost a lot of additional liquid. That's bad; it can't cope without water. You can last without food for a long time, but not without liquids. Keep quiet and don't move around. Someone will check up on you later. Do you want a rug?'

She gazed at him and mused that he was so multi-faceted. He acted like a macho man of the first rank sometimes, but he also had a compassionate streak. She looked at him. 'No, I'm fine. Know something? You're a nightmare on two legs most of the time, but at this moment, you're a hero. I'm extremely grateful. Thanks!'

He studied her silently for a second before he touched his peaked cap and gave her a smile that set her heartbeat scurrying to the outer corners of her consciousness. 'You're very welcome, princess.'

Whistling, he left her to it and ambled off along the wooden gangway in the direction of the wheelhouse.

9

Zoe heard a lot of activity on the other side of the boat and wondered what the others thought about her and her seasickness. She reminded herself to concentrate on the horizon. Fumbling for the handle of the mug, she picked it up and cradled it between her hands. It was still lukewarm. She took a tentative sip and hoped that it would stay down. Much to her surprise, after a while, the sickness did seem to fade a little.

★　★　★

Next morning she still couldn't face food, but to humour Billy she'd managed a couple of dried crackers at lunchtime. At first she couldn't even stand the smell of food, but it was getting better. The others teased her, but she accepted their rough humour. Maria remained reserved even though they now shared the same cabin.

Alex had vacated his own cabin for Maria's because his was bigger for the two girls. Zoe offered to sleep on the airbed and Maria didn't hesitate to nod her agreement. She still avoided talking to Zoe if she could. They hadn't really gelled from the start and Maria wanted to keep it that way.

The evening meal was over and everyone, including Zoe, was on deck. The engine was silent and the conversation circled and wandered back and forth. Zoe noted that Maria sat next to Alex, who was leaning against the bulkhead. She clearly felt she belonged there.

Zoe, on the edge of the group, leaned back and stared across the waters at the sunset. It was fantastic. The red, gold, orange and yellow tones intermingled on the surface of the sea. The evening sky and its reflected image in the water looked like a never-ending blazing fire. She glanced at the others and found

Alex was looking at her. It unsettled her and she told herself not to be silly. She remarked hurriedly, 'Isn't it beautiful?' She nodded towards the spectacle of the sunset. 'I've never seen anything more stunning. It's almost unreal.'

Alex leaned forward and rested his arms on his knees. 'Agreed! I don't think anyone ever experiences Caribbean sunsets without feeling floored. You forget all about the world and its countless problems and troubles, when you lean back with a can of cold beer and watch nature at its best.'

His T-shirt glowed in the semi-darkness. Zoe wrapped her arms around her knees and tried to commit the scene to memory. She realized that it was impossible. She wished she had her camera, but it was back at the hotel with all the other things. Billy told her that they'd radioed someone on Jost van Dyke, to tell Florence at the campground where she was. Balmy breezes blew from the water and enveloped the group relaxing on deck.

Zoe was one of the first to go below.

As she got ready for bed, she wondered how things would end. Everything was planned and calculated around the crew and not for an unexpected extra passenger. By the time she was ready, Maria joined her. Zoe decided to try and clear the air between them. If Maria had her sights on Alex and considered Zoe was a rival of some kind, she could put that right. Maria was welcome to him.

'Maria.'

With the beginnings of a sullen expression, Maria looked up. 'Yes, what do you want?'

With heightened colour, Zoe explained, 'In case you're worried, I'm not interested in Alex in a romantic way. I only met him because of my company investing money. I live in London and I'm staying there. I'm not his type of woman and he's not my kind of man, so please don't resent me for the wrong reasons. I'm not attracted to him and certainly have no intention of trying to attract him.'

Maria gave her a knowing smile. She pulled her T-shirt over her head. She wore nothing underneath as she headed for the bathroom. A few minutes later, she returned in a long-length T-shirt and cotton shorts. She began to ruffle among her clothes. She threw Zoe a floral bikini, some underwear and a pair of shorts. 'They should fit. You can't wear the same things all the time.'

It was Maria's peace offering and Zoe accepted it gratefully. 'Thanks. That's kind. Billy gave me a couple of his shrunken T-shirts this morning. They're too big, but they'll do.' Sounding almost cheerful, she said, 'I almost have a wardrobe of clothes again.'

'Tie a knot on the side.'

Zoe nodded. 'I know what you mean. That's a good idea. Like in the glossy magazines.' As Maria settled down in the bunk, Zoe said, 'I wish I was back on land.'

Maria shook her head and plumped her pillow. She sounded friendlier and more at ease. 'I think that depends on whether Alex can persuade this chap to sell him his gradiometer or not. If he doesn't, Alex may have to go back to the mainland to look for one, and then you'll have the chance to leave.'

'What's a gradiometer?'

'Basically it's something that collects underwater data and helps to locate any possible sites.'

Zoe plumped her pillow. 'Well, I don't know how I'm going to explain my absence to my boss if I'm not back on time. He won't believe it was just some kind of mix-up. My immediate boss is okay, but my boss's boss is a pain in the neck.'

Maria nodded. 'A lot of men are.'

Zoe bent her elbow and rested her head on her hand. Now that she was on talking terms with Maria, she boosted their tentative truce. 'Somehow I don't think that many men manage to get the better of you, do they?'

Maria laughed. 'No, not many. Some of them are hard nuts to crack, but I usually end up getting what I want. Not always though.' She turned onto her side and even managed to say, 'Goodnight.'

'Goodnight, Maria.' She punched her pillow into position and mused that Maria must want Alex very badly, if she'd felt jealous about another woman who wasn't even scheduled to remain part of the chosen team. He was an interesting, physically attractive man, but he was too complicated, too challenging and too difficult. Why did women get so het up about men like him in the first place? It must be sheer physical attraction. She hadn't met a man you could rely on for longer than a couple of weeks. These days, she took longer and longer to consider if someone was even worth going out with.

Lucy insisted she was too choosey. So far, her convictions hadn't improved things much. Her last boyfriend was cultured, well educated, refined and worked in the city. She'd met him in the beer garden of a pub where friends were celebrating a bachelor party. Zoe thought he was endearing and she grew fond of him. But she wanted love to be more breathtaking; to be something special. Spending weekends socializing with his refined parents and their equally refined friends in the country soon lost its attraction. He didn't understand that. They'd quarrelled about it, and finally parted as friends. They both recognized their feelings wouldn't last a lifetime. Zoe still hoped she'd find the perfect man, but slowly she was beginning to believe that he didn't exist. Some of her friends under thirty had married and were already divorced. She didn't want that. She decided one might as well stay single if the alternative was an artificial compromise, or a big mistake.

Next morning Zoe woke feeling more relaxed now that Maria wasn't spitting poison like a cobra. Her bunk was neatly made and bare. Zoe got ready leisurely. When she went on deck, she could tell the others were already busy. She made her way along the gangway to the galley. The movement of the waves still bothered her, but she didn't feel queasy anymore. There was still coffee in the machine, and bread lay next to the toaster. She could manage a piece of dry toast this morning. It tasted good. With her mug of coffee balanced carefully in one hand, she went back up on deck. The sky was bright blue and the water a mixture of blue and sapphire. The air was salty and invigorating. The wind whipped her T-shirt to her body. Underneath she wore Maria's bikini. She'd already washed her own underwear and hung it in the bathroom.

Sipping her coffee, she became aware of sounds on the other side of the boat. She strolled leisurely to the front of the boat, remembering that Billy told her to call it the bow and not the front. The crew were gathered around Alex, and he was shouting across to someone else on another boat drawn up alongside. Zoe watched silently.

From the look on Alex's face, things weren't going well. After a few minutes, the engine of the other boat revved and sped off. Alex and the others continued to discuss things. He'd pushed his peaked cap off his forehead and ran his hand down his tanned face.

Zoe turned away. She finished the coffee, swilled her mug out and went to fetch a towel. She may as well do a little sunbathing. She looked for a less prominent part of the deck. There wasn't much else for her to do anyway. She found a convenient spot between some coils of rope and a silent compressor. Lying there, hands behind her head, looking up at the deep blue of the sky, she imagined she was on a sundeck of a cruiser. After a while, a shadow fell across her and she shaded her eyes as she looked up. It was Alex.

He hitched his hands to his hips and Zoe could only picture how it would feel if those arms were around her. Long-neglected feelings made themselves known. He gave her body a raking glance and it sent shivers down her spine. The wind tousled his hair and she noticed that his face with its kissable mouth had a five o'clock shadow.

'It looks like you'll be back on the mainland later today, after all. That chap who just left has already sold what I wanted to someone else. I may be able to rent it back for a while if I find out where he is once we are back on shore.'

She sat up and felt a kind of relief to know that she would soon be far away from him again. He was a dangerous temptation. She wrapped her arms around her knees and stared up at him. 'I can't pretend I'm sorry your plans have been scuppered. It means I can leave for London on time.'

He laughed and it gave Zoe an unexpected warm feeling. 'Yes, but don't worry. I didn't aim to keep you on board anyway. I planned to dump you down the coast from your campground after we'd met this chap. We'll be able to take a direct route back. It'll take half the time.'

Trying to sound pleased, she said, 'Perhaps the gods are punishing you for keeping me on board. You had an unwanted, seasick passenger for twenty-four hours and didn't get your piece of equipment, so fate wasn't kind, was it?'

'True! But you survived and so will I.' He grinned. 'I have to get this search moving as soon as possible. Time is money. We'll be back in plenty of time for you to catch your plane.'

'I'm almost sorry to leave!' She waved her hand at the sea and the sky and confessed in a quieter voice, 'It's lovely. It's almost too good to be true. Now and then when we come in sight of an island and I see the sandy beaches and palm trees, I feel like pinching myself to find out if I'm really here.' She dared him to laugh at her. 'I suppose that sounds juvenile. People who come here for the first time doubtlessly all say the same thing.'

Zoe noticed that the initial amusement in his eyes softened to something nicer. 'It's not juvenile at all. I understand the sentiment completely. The Caribbean is one of my favourite places on earth.'

Zoe wanted to ask him about where the other places were, but she didn't. She felt awkward as his eyes travelled across her body again. She felt her pulse quicken and the colour in her face heightened. It meant nothing, of course. Assessing females was second nature to someone like him. She needed to disrupt his thoughts and say something sensible. 'Is there anything I can do to help? I feel a fraud just lazing around like a tourist.'

'The only thing everyone tries to avoid is their turn at cooking. Any good at that?'

'A matter of fact I quite like cooking. If my stomach can stand up to the smell, I'll try to rustle up the evening meal before I leave if you like.'

'Sounds good. Everyone is busy re-adjusting plans and fiddling around with their equipment again because of the delay. Take a look in the storeroom and the deep freeze, next to the galley.

See if you can find what you need.' He held out his hand and she hesitated before she took it and he dragged her up.

'I hope you've forgiven me for kidnapping you?'

His eyes grabbed all her attention. After a moment, she admitted, 'It was my own fault for falling asleep. Your reason for not having time to take me back was very plausible.'

He lifted his eyebrows and his lips twitched. 'But if I was a gentleman, I would still have given in to your request and turned the boat around.'

Her eyes sparkled and with pink cheeks, she replied, 'As I realize that you're no gentleman, I didn't really expect you to.' He chuckled. Something stopped her saying anything else that sounded too encouraging and friendly.

Viewing her, suddenly his fingers ran lightly across the curve of her shoulder. It took all of her self-control not to react. He remarked, 'I think you're heading for real trouble if you don't get out of the sun soon. Your skin is too fair to cope with too much sunshine too fast.'

His touch sent shivers down her spine. She swallowed hard and wanted to move away. Clear thoughts were impossible. She managed to cover her confusion by nodding and bending to grab her T-shirt. 'Till later then!' Zoe was glad to walk towards mid-ship and the galley.

He stood watching her. A hidden smile curved his mouth before he pulled on the peak of his cap and went to look for Billy.

10

Zoe made a good job of the spaghetti bolognese. She reasoned that a group of men needed plenty, so she made a large amount. They were all pleased with the result and when Alex tilted his head to the side and winked at her, she almost wished she could stay. Her defences were flimsy whenever he was around and she didn't want to show him how naïve she was in his presence. She'd be leaving them soon, and she was glad because she didn't know how best to react when he was close. Maria would scalp her if she only knew.

She went to stand at the bow of the ship and saw the mainland was already a thin line on the horizon. They were travelling at top speed. Alex wanted to get back quickly. The day's heat was fading and a balmy breeze flowed past her as she viewed the setting sun. She wished she could put it in a bottle and take it home. On a dreary winter day, it would be wonderful to remove the cork and relive this moment.

Billy came past and chatted for a few minutes, then she was alone again, watching the mainland grow closer, until Alex joined her. Zoe felt how her heart suddenly raced in nervous anticipation. It was the last time they'd be alone. She tensed and hung on even more tightly to the railing.

He stood beside her and when she glanced across, he was watching her. She noticed how his eyes narrowed and then looked away into the distance. He smiled in an almost affectionate way. 'Not much longer now, then you can scuttle off to your mosquito-infested cabin.'

'I hope I never scuttle anywhere. That would be undignified. Although I admit, in one way I'm sorry to leave.'

The amusement in Alex's eyes was infectious. 'Can I dare hope you'll miss me?'

'Don't be big-headed! I'll miss the sunset, the sea, the sky, and all of the crew.'

'When will I see you again?'

She shrugged. 'Who knows? You'll be busy having a successful search for treasure, and I'll be sweating away at my desk in London.' She brushed some strands of hair out of her face.

His eyes lit up. 'In that case . . . ' He suddenly reached out for her and pulled her towards him. She was so close she felt they were moulded together. His breath fanned her face and then his lips touched hers. Zoe had no will of her own. The kiss automatically wakened devils within her and made her want more of him. He tasted salty and enticing. Instinctively she knew his kiss was the one she'd always yearned for. It was a promise of pleasures unknown. Even if she'd tried to ignore that, the feeling of the solid bulk and strength of his body made her insides tingle.

She breathed heavily and steadied her racing pulse. His physical attractions, and her reaction to them, were blocking any sensible behaviour. She ran her tongue over her lips and tried to pull back. 'Why did you do that?'

'An impulse.' There was laughter in his pale grey eyes. He shrugged.

Trying to sound unruffled, she said, 'I expect kissing someone means nothing to you, but I prefer to kiss people I like.' She stared into his light grey eyes. Zoe guessed he was a man who'd undoubtedly done a lot more than just kiss other women. She didn't want to mull that over but it was there, eating away at her inner being. In all likelihood, he presumed she was just waiting to melt into his arms.

He contemplated her for a moment and murmured, 'So do I.'

She was caught unawares when he pulled her towards him again. This time his kiss was even more possessive and demanding. Their closeness left her in no doubt about what he was thinking. For a moment, she wanted to give in and she locked her fingers behind his head. He lifted an eyebrow. He said in a rough voice, 'Somehow I think you do like me, even though you fight against it.' As he uttered the phrase, his mouth wandered down to the neckline of her blouse.

Zoe knew she was enjoying the experience, but her subconscious warned her of the danger. She yanked away. She was too inexperienced to get involved with Alex Harding. He'd wrap her round his little finger in minutes, and make her want him in a way she could only imagine. Confused, she turned sharply and hurried down the steps to the lower deck. Her hand was already on the handrail when he called after her.

'I never thought you were a quitter.'

'I'm not. I'm just choosey.'

The sound of a muted chuckle wafted on the air to follow her down the steps.

She reminded herself that he collected women like other men collected stamps. There was no emotion involved. Alex Harding thought women were just there to please men. She hoped for Maria's sake that she didn't expect too much of him. He was someone who gave as much as he wanted to. No more, no less. It was just as well they wouldn't meet again. There was no future in dallying with someone like him.

★ ★ ★

When Zoe emerged later, Alex was no longer in sight. The ship was already manoeuvring into position next to the quay. She said goodbye hurriedly to the others and hoped to disembark without seeing Alex again, but he was suddenly standing behind her. She felt hot and cold. Part of her wanted to lean away from him and the rest wanted to sink into the warmth of his arms again. The impact he'd made in just a few days was quite ridiculous. She had to escape from him and all this pondering and reflection.

She turned and held out her hand. Trying to sound calm and collected, she said, 'Thanks for bringing me back safely and also for acting as my personal nurse.'

He held her hand a trifle too long and then pushed his cap farther up his forehead. 'No trouble, princess. Have a safe journey home. You'll hear from me as soon as I have something worth reporting.'

She nodded. Judging accurately the swell of the water, she jumped onto the pier and walked determinedly towards the main road. She didn't look back as she marched to the campground. It only took her a few minutes to reach her cabin. She was safe at last.

Early next morning, Florence brought Zoe's breakfast and chatted to her as if it were a normal occurrence that one of her guests disappeared, and then reappeared three days later.

Zoe found she had no time to play tourist. She had to hurry to get the connecting transport she needed to get her to the international airport for her flight back to London.

11

George viewed Zoe from the other side of his desk. 'So it looked okay to you?'

Zoe nodded. 'As far as I can tell. The boat was in excellent condition, and the people he's chosen are good at their jobs.'

'You've caught a bit of sun.'

She flashed him a smile. 'Have I? That's surprising, since I spent at least one day below deck, being seasick.' Zoe cringed inwardly as she recalled how Alex had played nursemaid.

He nodded. 'You don't have to be on the ocean to feel sick. One of our kids can't manage the trip to the local supermarket without retching.'

Absentmindedly, Zoe commented, 'Try boiled ginger before you set out. That helps.'

'Ginger? I'll tell my wife. So . . . I suppose we now have to wait and see what comes of it all. William will scalp me if his money goes down the drain.'

She raised an eyebrow. 'If he does, hint that you know all about the hidden account. He'll soon shut up.' Zoe didn't want to think about losing her own money. Lucy would never let her forget, but no one else apart from the company lawyer knew, thank goodness.

'Alex Harding promised to keep you informed?'

'Yes, but I don't know when, where or how. I don't know how bad or good communications are, wherever he's going. If I hear anything, I'll pass it on, straight away.'

★ ★ ★

That evening Lucy called around with a giant pizza. Her hips moved provocatively in a skimpy black skirt, patterned stockings, a pair of trendy high heels, a bright turquoise sweater, and lots of chunky jewellery. Zoe knew her matching skirt and top in neutral colours must look drab in contrast, but she realized a leopard couldn't change its spots, and it was all a matter of taste. People always said she looked smart, and she felt at ease with herself, so there was no reason to feel bad about their differing styles.

Bustling around in Zoe's small kitchen, Lucy arranged some plates and cutlery on the breakfast bar. She patted the neighbouring stool as she wiggled onto the other one and reached for a bottle of red wine. 'Come on, tell me all about it! Every single detail. What were the steel bands like? Did you like the food? What were the men like? Any talent? I expected you'd come back with a glorious bronzed body. Any tan you had is already fading.'

Zoe sat down. 'I didn't see or hear a single steel band! There was some reggae music one evening via a stereo in the middle of bottles on a shelf. They had a local cocktail, though, called pain killer. It was very good.'

'What?' Pausing in mid-air from

tucking into her pizza, Lucy looked up, mystified. 'You were in the land of steel bands and hunky sunburnt bodies for a week. How could you fail to hear music, and stop your body moving in rhythm? I packed you that purple mini-skirt with all the beading. It was perfect for nights out in the local bar.'

Zoe attacked her pizza and between mouthfuls she told her friend what had happened.

Looking suitably astonished, Lucy said, 'You got trapped on board ship? Just like that?' Her surprised expression changed to worry. 'Nothing awful happened, I hope? This chap didn't try anything on, did he? You read such scary stories about what happens to single female tourists when they're abroad.'

Zoe shook her head. 'No, it was all harmless and entirely my own fault. I fell asleep, and they didn't find me until they were far out to sea.' With traces of nervousness, she added, 'I did ask Alex to take me back, but he refused because he was on his way to meet someone. He said he just didn't have time to turn around.'

'How long were you on board? How many men?'

'Almost three days. Four men, including Alex, and one other woman.'

'At least there was another female. What did you do apart from sunbathing?'

'It's a working boat, not a cruiser. I was sick as a dog one day. They didn't want me on board and were glad to get rid of me when we returned to shore. I cooked for them the final evening. Apart from that I lazed around and wished I was on the mainland instead of trapped on a boat.'

Munching away, Lucy remarked, 'I looked up Alex Harding on the internet and found a couple of pictures. He looks yummy. I wouldn't mind being shipwrecked on a desert island with him.'

Pushing bits of pizza round her plate, Zoe replied, 'You're welcome! He's over-confident and a womanizer into the bargain.'

'Aha! I can tell he impressed you.'

Zoe took a nervous sip of her drink. 'As a planner and manager he's first-rate, but I think he's a bit of a wolf.' Zoe decided not to mention the kiss. It meant nothing, and if Lucy heard about it, she'd face never-ending questions of when, how, and why.

'What a pity. I had hopes of going shopping for a wedding dress.'

'You're incorrigible,' Zoe said, laughing. 'I don't want someone I can't trust. Maria, the woman on board, thinks he's wonderful, but I couldn't figure out how chummy they were. They were close, but I missed the physical signs.'

'It's about time you had someone to stir your emotions. Your last boyfriend was a nerd. Clive's idea of excitement was spending the afternoon on a riverbank catching unsuspecting fish, wasn't it?'

Zoe nodded. 'That or visiting his parents. He thought fishing was electrifying fun. To be honest, it was very relaxing after a busy week in the office.

I fell asleep most of the time.'

'Exactly! You can do that when you've been married ten years, but not when you're still young and healthy and need passion.'

'I'm beginning to think men are just more trouble than they're worth,' Zoe said, running her fingers through her hair.

'Shows how differently we think. I think they're like a wonderful bag of liquorice allsorts. You have to keep tasting all the flavours, and then one day you find you're mad about just one of them.'

★   ★   ★

A day or so later, an incoming email stated, 'Contacting you at home this evening — 8 p.m., urgent. A.'

Zoe looked at the sender's address but it meant nothing to her. She was about to put it in the trash bin when she wondered if 'A' stood for Alex. How many As did she know, and how many would be so blunt? She printed it out and deleted the original message from her computer. She was curious for the rest of the day.

That evening when her computer heralded an email, she glanced at the address and noted it was the same one as earlier. The message read:

'Hi Zoe, I suspect that someone is on our trail, hoping we'll lead them to the treasure so that they can bag it for themselves. I need your help. Someone I know can supply software to block signals to or from the boat. It'll take too long for it to get here by airmail or by any other method. I'd like you to bring it personally, straight away. Provided you agree to help, I'll sort it out with your boss tomorrow and explain how urgent it is. If we block signals, it'll be hard for anyone to follow us.

'I'll ask my friend to bring it to your office. He'll be a scruffy-looking individual with a beard and red hair,

but he's a whiz with a computer. You don't need to worry about payment. There isn't anyone locally I could use to do the same work, and I can't afford to waste time. There's no danger involved, so don't get hysterical. I'm waiting here for your reply. — .'

Zoe read the message twice and was gobsmacked. Her boss wouldn't agree to her winging her way across the Atlantic again, but Alex seemed to think otherwise. She didn't even want to go. She'd prefer to ignore Alex if possible. The kiss hadn't meant a thing to him, but she'd been on the brink of demonstrating that she was his for the taking. Was she strong enough to resist if he tried again? She didn't want to end up with a damaged heart. She ordered her wandering thoughts and returned to the computer keyboard.

'I do not scare easily and I'm not a hysterical woman. Where are you?

Why can't your friend deliver it personally? — Z.'

'He is a computer genius, but he is useless in day-to-day life. If I asked him to bring it, he'll end up wandering around Greenland wondering what he was doing there. He joined the motorway via the exit slipway once and caused chaos till the police got him off. He'd never make it to the right plane or the right country. He depends on taxis to get him to even mundane destinations. I'm depending on you. I'm mailing from a friend's computer in Jamaica. — A.'

'What about the air fare? I'm not a millionaire. All this flitting back and forth across the Atlantic may be routine for you, it's not for me. — Z.'

'If you come, I'll arrange for a ticket to be waiting at the airport. It all comes out of the kitty. — A.'

She paused before she finally wrote,

'*Where do we meet? — Z.*'

'*Good girl! You fly to Antigua like last time. I'll be there to pick you up. If I can't make it for some reason, I'll send Billy. Same flight, same day. I'll contact the chap about the software straight away. He's been working on the problem for a few days already. His name is Andrew. You can't mistake him. We called him Carrot at school — you'll soon see why. I'll be in touch again after I've talked to your boss and I'll let you know where to collect the ticket etc. Thanks for agreeing. — A.*'

Zoe didn't know how to end their exchange, so she just leaned back and studied the words there. She wondered if she was going crazy. He seemed to think he could organize her, her boss, this unknown computer whiz, and anyone else, without batting an eyelid.

Somehow, she began to realize that he could.

★   ★   ★

Billy met her in Antigua. He explained that the *Astrea* was moored a couple of nautical miles offshore and they'd get there with the ship's dinghy. Half an hour later, they were on board ship again. Hank was carrying a heavy crate and shouted a cheerful 'hello' before he carried on. Zoe prayed she wouldn't be seasick again. This time she'd brought some tablets and had ginger-water in a thermos flask.

Maria emerged from below deck and when she saw Zoe, she gave her a nod and a wary smile. Zoe could imagine men would find her extremely attractive. She looked exotic, interesting, beautiful, and she was clever too.

Hoping to sound friendly, Zoe said, 'Hi, Maria. How are things?'

Maria nodded and sounded friendly for a change. 'Fine. We're sharing the cabin again, but we've a camp-bed this time, so one of us doesn't have to sleep on the hard floor.'

Zoe thought she would just deliver the software and then leave straight away, but clearly Alex had made other plans. 'I'll take the camp-bed. You're entitled to the proper bed. You're a crew member. I'm just ballast.'

'Hi, Zoe!' Alex's voice wakened her entire awareness of him, and she wished she didn't react so pathetically at the mere sound of his presence. She spun around and wondered how long he'd been there. Forcing herself to face him and hoping she appeared calm and unruffled, she replied, 'Hello, Alex.'

His eyes raked her briefly. 'Journey okay? Any problems?'

'No, everything went like clockwork, including Billy waiting for me when I came through customs control.'

'You brought the software?'

'Yes. Do you want it straight away? Your friend is a strange man, isn't he? He looks helpless and bewildered, but actually he's very endearing. He reminds me of a lost puppy.'

Alex laughed briefly. 'Yes, Andrew lives in a world of his own, but he's a good guy and a genius with a computer. Computer technology is the world he understands, loves and lives in. His sister keeps an eye on him, otherwise he'd forget to eat. I'll be grateful if you bring me the software as soon as you've unpacked. The sooner we do all we can to stop these people following us, or at least slow them down, the better.'

She fumbled in her bag and handed him a memory stick and an envelope. 'He said it's all stored on that and he included some written tips and instructions in case you get into difficulties while installing it. I still think it was a waste of time and money for me to come all this way just for that, though.'

'I needed someone I trusted to do it and I needed it fast. You were the obvious choice.'

She swallowed a lump in her throat. His remark was nothing special. 'What does the software do?'

'Like I told you in my mail, it blocks signals unless I allow them through. If no one can pick up radio, sonar, instrument or cell-phone signals, we can't be positioned so easily. They might be able to pick up a ship's outlines, but it'll take much longer to establish which ship. If we change position constantly, it'll be pretty difficult to follow us. Anyway, that's what I'm hoping.'

'You mentioned you thought you were being pursued? By rivals for the treasure?'

He shrugged. 'I can't think of anyone else who'd bother. I've delayed sailing to the actual search area until I had this software. They'll need to keep within sight to tail the *Astrea*, and that'll help us to keep moving and avoiding them.'

'I thought the search was registered, and only you have the legal rights to anything you find.'

'That doesn't mean there aren't crooks out there just waiting to pounce.'

'You don't need me anymore now, do

you? I could fly home again in a day or so.'

'Perhaps, but I'd like to leave immediately. We've lost enough time hanging around here already. Taking you back to the mainland will take too long. I've cleared things with your boss, and a couple of days in the sun wouldn't come amiss, will it? We can drop you off in a couple of days' time. We're bound to run out of something and need to pull into port somewhere.'

She tilted her head. 'I'm wondering what you told William. He isn't usually very generous about unofficial leave.'

His eyes twinkled. 'I think I scared him when he heard my theory of outsiders wanting to grab the booty. I hinted it was a good idea for you to keep your eyes on the crew for a while just in case one of them was a bad apple. He took the bite. I think he was terrified that we'd cheat him, and ultimately he was happy you'll be here to play watchdog.'

She shook her head. 'Poor William.

He didn't have a chance, did he? And what am I supposed to do, apart from soaking up the sun every day?'

'I talked to the others, and we agreed we're very keen on you being our cook for as long as you're on board. None of us like cooking apart from Hank, and his accomplishments are dishes of baked beans with anything that fits the frying pan. Have you ever had fish with baked beans? It's awful! In comparison your spaghetti bolognese went down a treat.'

With wide eyes she stuttered, 'Cooking? Me? I'm not a cook.'

'You're a five-star cook in comparison to the rest of us. Come on, Zoe. I even bought a cookery book for you, just in case.'

'Gee, thanks! That's a wonderful prospect, sweating in the galley every day.'

He reached forward and ruffled her hair. 'It's one of the most important jobs. A contented crew works well, and a contented crew loves decent food.'

Maria laughed. 'Alex, you may be in charge, but you could at least give her the chance to say no if she doesn't want to do it. She's not used to rough seafarers.'

His pale grey eyes considered her and he remained silent. Zoe gave in. She didn't mind cooking and it would give her something to do if she was on board ship for a couple of days. It sounded like the boat would return to the mainland for new supplies quite soon and then she'd leave them to it. It'd be interesting to watch the search for a while.

She looked at him. 'Okay, I'll give it a try. There's no guarantee that you'll like what I make, but it's on your own head.'

His mouth turned up at the corner. 'Great.' He waved the memory stick and the envelope in the air. 'I'll sort this out right away. That means you have time to settle down before we raise the anchor and actually leave.'

12

The next couple of days were good. Zoe was on holiday during the day and enjoyed making simple but tasty dishes using Alex's cookery book in the evenings. Lots of kitchen aids were missing but she was good at adapting. She always enjoyed cooking, but seldom cooked these days. Cooking for one wasn't much fun.

Lazing and soaking up the sun the rest of the time, she noticed the men bantered among themselves like any other group of men who knew each other well, but Alex often curbed their use of bad language when he noticed the women were within earshot.

The sky was cloudless, the air was warm, and the turquoise water was like silk as it flowed over Zoe's body when they went swimming. Alex wanted to get to the search area as fast as he could, but early in the morning and when darkness was descending the ship bobbed silently on the gentle water and everyone jumped overboard. After she'd used up her energy, Zoe sometimes sat with her legs dangling over the side, watching the others in the water. Alex looked tough, lean and sinewy in his swimming gear, and his powerful well-muscled body moved with easy grace through the waves. All the men had strong, brawny bodies but Alex had an athletic physique with no extra weight. When everybody came on board again they usually sat in a friendly group for a while, chatting and enjoying the time together. They were all more or less captivated by the atmosphere and the surroundings. Sharing impressions and leisure time made everything even more meaningful.

Zoe decided that if Maria and Alex were having an affair, they were very discreet about it. During the daytime, she noticed their moments of extra familiarity and how relaxed they were with each other, but their gestures were never so intimate that Zoe or the others felt uncomfortable. She tried not to pay them special attention but didn't always succeed.

The men liked to tease her about her lack of nautical knowledge, but she took it in good stead. She was grateful that this time she hadn't been seasick. She was also glad that she was responsible for a cooked meal every evening, otherwise she'd feel completely superfluous. Breakfast was always hassle-free. Whoever was first in the galley made the coffee. Everyone helped himself, or herself, to whatever else they wanted, whenever they wanted it.

Zoe was sitting on deck one morning admiring the colours of the sunrise when Maria, busy with a job nearby, asked, 'Do you mind doing the cooking?'

'No, not really. It gives me something to do. My gran was a good cook. I spent a lot of time with her when I was small. I watched and learned from her. I wouldn't like to do it professionally, but I enjoy trying to make a decent meal.'

'Rather you than me. I never liked cooking. That was one of the things my husband criticized, all the time. He took it for granted that all women could cook and liked doing so. He also had a lot of other firm notions about what women should or shouldn't do.'

Taken aback, Zoe said, 'Your husband? You're married? I didn't know that.'

Maria stared out across the water. 'I was. Luckily, I'm not anymore. We were divorced six months ago, although he's still a bloody big nuisance.'

'Oh!'

Maria gripped her mug even tighter and Zoe could see the white of her knuckles. She decided not to prod any further. Maria didn't offer more information, and Zoe didn't intend to destroy their tentative friendship by asking unwelcome questions.

After a pause, Maria brushed the wind-blown hair out of her face and continued. 'Yes, he was the biggest mistake of my life.' She looked towards the men busy at the other end of the ship. 'What about you? Is there a significant man in your life?'

'No. I keep on thinking I'll meet someone special one day, but it hasn't happened. The only man I really fancied goes back to when I was at university. I thought he was special, but I wasn't clever enough to spot that I wasn't the only one in his life. I was content to be his lapdog until I found out I was only one of many. That's made me very cautious, and suspicious. I don't intend to make the same mistake again. I'd rather stay single.'

Sounding surprised and shocked, Maria said, 'You've never had a boyfriend since then? That must be years ago.'

Zoe laughed. 'Of course I have, but only a couple of fleeting affairs with men I thought might be different. They always ended as downright disappointments. Too many men these days think life is just a jungle, and they are the hunters. I don't want my head hanging on the wall as one of their hunting trophies.'

'I know what you mean. I made a hell of a mistake when I chose my husband.' She threw back her head and her hair rippled down her back. 'There are some good men around if you're lucky enough to find them.'

Zoe nodded silently. It was easy for Maria to say that. Alex and Maria were already pairing off. 'Perhaps you're right. I don't know. I'm sure that I'm better off without someone if he ends up making my life a misery in the long run.'

'You're right. It's difficult to find a good man.' Maria looked along the deck. 'I'd better join the others and make sure they don't shove any of my equipment where I can't find it later.'

The discussion was on safe ground again, and Zoe responded, 'I'm surprised how much work there is all the time. Everyone's constantly busy.'

Maria lifted her shoulders. 'Yes. You keep checking, checking, preparing and inspecting. Once we get to the right place, we won't have much time for more than routine checks. Everything has to be perfect when Hank, Gary, or Alex start to dive. Things like the blower platform have to function perfectly. Until yesterday even that wasn't fixed, but it is now. I'd better join them, and see if they need help with something else.'

She sauntered off, coffee mug in hand, and a minute later, Zoe heard her joining in the men's conversation. Maria fitted into this man's world effortlessly. She'd grown up among divers and salvage workers.

Zoe cleared the galley, filled the coffee machine and then went to look for her paperback. She plastered herself with sun blocker, grabbed some thick towels and her sunglasses, and looked for a shady spot. As soon as she'd made herself comfortable between some harmless-looking drums, she slipped her hands under her head, looked up at some noisy seabirds circling far above, and noticed how the warm winds were ruffling the rigging. If there were seabirds, that meant they were in flying distance of the mainland. This time she didn't long to be there; she was grateful to be right here, right now.

★   ★   ★

It had been another great day, and it had taken longer than usual to clear the small galley this evening. Before Zoe went below, she leaned on the railings and stared out across the sea. Moonlight was dancing like sparks of diamonds on the waves, and the balmy air lifted her hair and caressed her neck. Billy and Hank were talking softly on the other side of the ship with cans of beer. Gary and Maria had gone below straight after the end of the meal.

'Hey! I thought you hadn't gone below yet. Like a can of beer?'

Alex's voice made her insides turn to

jelly because she wasn't expecting him. It only showed her how vulnerable she was. It was just as well she'd be leaving them when they put into port for something they needed.

She nodded and he must have had one ready, because he handed it to her. She flipped the seal and it fizzed; then she took a long, cool gulp. 'Um! Just what I needed.' She concentrated on the swell of the water and its gentle swishing as it hit the body of the ship. They stood in companionable silence and finished their beers in measured sips. She turned and squeezed the can out of shape before returning her attention to the sea.

'You haven't had any trouble with seasickness this time? You're turning into a real sea-dog.'

She laughed softly. 'Not so far, anyway. I do drink some of Billy's ginger water now and then, if I feel queasy. I brought travel-sickness tablets with me but I haven't needed them yet.'

He came to stand next to her. This

was too close for her peace of mind, but she couldn't move away without seeming rude. He leaned on the railing and bent forward, looking down into the water. 'Good. Thanks for doing the cooking, Zoe. We all appreciate it even if we don't shower you with praise.'

Zoe was glad the shadows hid the colour rising in her cheeks. 'You're welcome. At least I don't feel completely worthless.'

'You'd never be worthless, whatever you did.'

'Are you just flattering me, so that I'll make your favourite dish tomorrow?'

'I'm not flattering you.' He straightened. 'I do like to tease you, but I take you seriously too. I always have.'

It was hard to remain coherent, so she shrugged to hide her confusion and started to turn away. He halted her escape with a firm hand on her arm. Cupping her chin with the other, he searched her upturned face in the shadows and then gently pressed his lips to hers. His kiss left her weak and confused. Her lips were still warm and moist from his kiss when he brushed another gentle kiss across her forehead and then turned her and gave her a gentle push. 'Go to bed, Zoe, before it gets too complicated.'

She had to block an impulse to run. She forced herself to turn away and walk to the steps leading below deck. Out of sight, she leaned back and brushed her lips with the back of her hand. At first, she wondered if it was merely a 'thank-you' kiss, but it was too passionate for that. She'd longed to forget her vow not to show she liked him. It would've been easy to forget reality and let go. She felt a magnetic pull towards him, even though she knew it was futile. Thank heavens he'd broken off. He was already paired with Maria, and that meant he was off-bounds for her. Perhaps he had other girlfriends waiting elsewhere. If that was so, either Maria didn't know about it or she didn't care. Perhaps Maria was prepared to accept whatever he offered without questions.

When Zoe got to the cabin, Maria was already asleep. She slipped into bed quietly. Like Maria, she now wore shorts and T-shirts to sleep in. Sexy pyjamas or nightdresses were out of place because they usually went on deck first thing in the morning to take in the freshness before dressing properly. She slept without covering; it was too hot for that.

She lay in the darkness unable to sleep. She stared up at the ceiling and thought about Alex, almost wishing she wasn't here, but far away from him. He was a danger to her peace of mind. There was a real risk that if he persuaded her to accept whatever he was prepared to give, it would be a meaningless affair. That wasn't the kind of love she wanted. She tossed and turned and finally fell into a disturbed slumber.

She was woken rudely. Someone had one hand over her mouth and was pinning her to the bed with the other.

She heard scuffling from Maria's bunk bed and saw the shadow of another man there. The two of them were muttering, and he tied a handkerchief clumsily round her mouth. It had happened so fast and she wanted to scream, but he had the handkerchief in place and knotted before Zoe had the chance. She was still confused and muddled when he pulled her upright and tied her hands behind her back. She couldn't think clearly and saw Maria was facing the same predicament. The men pushed them out of the cabin, along the gangway and up the steps. Was she dreaming? What was going on?

Zoe prayed someone on board would hear them and look, but no one did. She remembered how she'd often heard people moving around the deck during the night if they couldn't sleep. She'd just turned over and taken no notice.

Once on deck, they jostled them to the side and half-pushed, half-lowered them into a dinghy. A third man waited for them there. Once they'd dumped the women on the floor of the small boat, no one paid them much attention anymore. The three men took up the oars and pulled away from Alex's ship with powerful strokes. Zoe thought briefly about slipping over the side into the water, but knew that was a stupid, fruitless idea. Her hands were tied and she'd sink to the bottom and drown.

As soon as they were out of earshot, the men started the outboard motor. They sped over the water for a while until they reached a bigger ship that looked dark and threatening in the gloomy light. The two women were bundled up a short rope ladder. Someone hauled them onto the deck, and amid excited voices, they were taken below deck. Pushed along a gloomy gangway, they were finally shoved into an airless, stuffy cabin. One man cut the rope around their wrists and left them standing, locking the door behind him.

13

Zoe wrenched the handkerchief off her mouth and rubbed her wrists. She looked at Maria and saw the other woman's frightened eyes. Did she herself look like that? Probably. She was afraid, although she tried not to show it, and she didn't want to panic. With a dry throat, she spluttered, 'Do you know what this is all about?'

Maria's face was white. She shook her head and her voice trembled a little. 'Perhaps they're the people who've been following Alex.'

'But why take us?'

Maria's voice continued to sound jittery. 'Perhaps they hope to pressure Alex into agreeing to their demands. They can haggle better if they have us in their power. I wonder how they knew we were on board.'

Still feeling dumbfounded, Zoe remarked,

'This is the twenty-first century. Men can't just grab women. Pirates did, centuries ago, but there aren't any pirates anymore.'

'There are revolutionaries. Have you never read about rebels hijacking innocent people, in South America?'

Zoe rubbed her wrists. 'I don't believe this. I'm not officially a member of the crew. I shouldn't be here. My company just gave Alex some investment money.' Sounding more assured than she felt, she declared, 'This is a crime and it's not funny.'

Maria was regaining some of her customary confidence too and gave a soft chuckle. 'Try telling them that. It was carefully planned and they knew exactly where to find us. Someone must have watched the *Astrea* closely. We can only hope that Alex and the others notice we're missing and make a deal with these people, otherwise we'll probably end up on the bottom of the sea as fish food.'

A shiver ran down Zoe's spine and

she flopped down on a nearby chair. 'I just can't believe this is happening to me! I've been kidnapped!'

The two of them went on talking about the situation while scrutinizing the cabin and waiting for something else to happen. For a long time nothing did. The sun was up when they heard footsteps in the corridor outside. Tensing, they instinctively drew together and stood side by side. When it opened, one man waited outside while another one entered and gave them a suffocating, oily smile.

He looked Mexican. His jet-black hair was greasy and unkempt, and it looked like he'd slept in his grubby clothes. His teeth were yellow and he had stubble on his chin. 'Good morning, ladies! Welcome to our little ship. We hope your stay will be brief and uneventful. Nothing will happen to you, as long as you remain cooperative.'

Trying to sound confident, Zoe said, 'Why are we here? Who are you? Take us back to out friends immediately.

You'll face long prison sentences if you don't.'

'Prison?' His eyes glittered. 'It would be your word against ours. In our version, you wanted us to rescue you. You came of your own free will.'

'Don't be ridiculous. Why should we?'

He stroked his beard-shadowed chin. 'Who knows? Perhaps the men were molesting you and you needed to escape. Perhaps they refused to let you go, and you managed to signal to us. Anyhow, I'm just telling you to cooperate. You'll stay until we've settled the deal.'

'What deal?'

'You'll find out soon enough. Just keep quiet and do as you are told.'

Zoe saw he didn't intend to explain what was going on. Nothing made much sense, but it looked like they had no choice. 'It's already stifling in this cabin and it's going to get worse later in the day. We need some fresh air.'

He strode past them, leaving a trail of exotic smells in his wake. He wrenched at the rusty fastening securing the small porthole. Under protest, it gave way, and the open porthole let in the sea breeze. He gestured toward it. 'My pleasure. Your air-conditioning system for your stay with us. Someone will bring you something to eat and drink soon. Don't try any tricks or you'll be sorry.'

Maria retorted, 'You're the one who's going to be sorry.'

He gave her a long, hard stare. 'Ah, the beautiful Maria. I've heard a lot about you.' His eyes raked her body.

Zoe decided she needed to side-track his attention. 'We need clean water, and what about a toilet?'

He nodded towards a door on the side. 'That's the bathroom. You'll get drinking water in bottles. Use the bathroom water for everything else. You, see ladies, we've thought of your comfort down to the last detail. We hope that your stay with us will be short. I expect you do too.' He turned on his heel and left them.

Zoe guessed that they didn't intend them any bodily harm — not at the moment anyway. She could afford to call after him, 'Go fly a kite, you hoodlum!'

They heard the key turning in the lock again. Standing silently, they looked at one another and listened to the departing heavy footsteps and the sound of men laughing.

14

Alex arched his back and stretched his arms above his head. Maria's bunk was too narrow and too short for his frame. He gazed across the water. It looked like another perfect day ahead and they were nearing the search site. He felt a lot happier since he'd got the software to block unwarranted signals. They'd reach their destination soon. No one on board was up yet; it was the best part of any day. A few moments on his own to consider things that bothered him, before the day-to-day business flowed over him.

Staring ahead, he admitted that the fact that Zoe was dragging her feet bothered him. They both felt the attraction, but she was wary and didn't trust him. He ran his hand down his face. Perhaps someone had been feeding her with stories about his past.

True, he had played the field ever since Diana had let him down. But now that he'd met Zoe, he felt his defences crumbling and something in him had changed. He wanted to spend time with her and get to know her better. She wasn't the type for a quick trip between the sheets. The animal attraction was definitely there, but it wasn't the only thing he felt this time. As well as wanting her physically, he simply enjoyed her company and their conversations, and he wanted her to like him. He couldn't remember when he'd last felt that way about a woman.

Zoe was obviously drawing her own conclusions about Maria's place in his life. That was problematic. He'd promised to keep his mouth shut and take care of Maria. He didn't want to break his word, but he wanted to tell Zoe the truth. Between them, Maria and he played the part well enough. It convinced someone like Zoe. He could tell by the way she looked and acted that she'd paired them off in her mind.

They didn't need to bill and coo all the time. If they smiled often and gave each other extra attention, it was enough. Trouble was, it was a farce. He wanted to be honest with Zoe, or they'd never get together. He'd have a word with Maria and the others and see if they thought it was safe to tell her the whole story.

Billy came lumbering along the gangway. He looked at Alex and then at the colours of the morning, as the sun took over for the day. 'Don't think I'll ever get used to it. After working most of my life in the cold, grey North Sea, this is paradise.' He wasn't a sentimental or emotional man, but the colours and the atmosphere of the Caribbean had captured his imagination.

Alex nodded. 'Yes, it's easy to understand why the rich and famous buy an island and settle here, isn't it?'

Billy looked around. 'Where's everyone this morning? Hank was about to emerge when I left, and I know Gary has gone straight to check the engine.

Where are the two girls? Maria planned to check the compressor with me this morning. Zoe is usually up by now too. She wasn't in the galley when I popped my head around the door. I actually look forward to our meals since she's in charge. Even the coffee tastes better.'

Alex grinned. 'Yes, that's true. Perhaps they're busy with girl-talk and forgot the time. They get on better than they did when Zoe first came on board. I'm glad. It'd be hell if we had two women bickering and squabbling all the time.'

Billy rubbed his chin. 'Zoe isn't the squabbling type. I like her. She has a calming effect on the people round her because, despite the fact that she's confident, she's a very friendly character. In comparison Maria is a bag of fireworks; you never know when she'll explode. The two of them are getting along better now though.'

Alex nodded, but didn't comment.

'Maria is good at playing the besotted girlfriend, isn't she?'

Alex ran his hand over his face. 'I was just thinking about talking to all of you about that. When she arrived, I thought it was better to keep Zoe ignorant of the truth in case she unwittingly passed on the information later back on land. I think we know her well enough now to know she wouldn't spill the beans.' Billy nodded. 'It's up to Maria. I'll talk to her about Zoe and see what she thinks.' He straightened. 'I'm going to check the route again. If we're lucky, we might reach our target area today.'

The lines on Billy's forehead deepened. 'We still need to keep checking other ships. They could be innocent, or they could be someone who's trying to follow us.'

An hour later, Billy had finished his daily tasks and went to the galley. To his surprise, everything was still empty and silent. He scratched his head and went to the bridge. Alex was bent over some charts with a pencil and notebook.

'Hey — something's wrong. There's still no sign of the women.'

Alex looked up and smiled. 'Why do you always imagine the worst possible scenario?' He threw the pencil down and led the way. Outside they met Hank.

Hank said, 'Just went for coffee. There's no one there. Is Zoe seasick again?'

Billy shook his head. 'We haven't seen Maria this morning either. We're just on our way to find out where they are.'

Below, Alex knocked softly on the door. He got no answer. He tried again, louder this time. There was still no reaction. He pushed the door open. They noted the disarrayed bedclothes. Alex's eyes swept the cabin. 'Perhaps they've gone for a swim and forgotten to tell someone?'

Hank picked up a sheet of paper from the bed. He read it and handed it to Alex. 'It's nothing as simple as a morning swim. Someone has kidnapped them and we didn't notice a thing.'

A tense silence enveloped the room as Alex read the message and passed it to Billy. 'Yes, that's it in a nutshell. I wonder who they are. Where the hell did they take them? They seem to know Maria, because they mention her name. They don't mention Zoe, so I wonder if she just got in the way. If they're treasure-hunters, they may be hoping to blackmail us into giving them the booty in exchange for the women.' He spoke quietly as if he was still testing the idea in his brain. His eyes narrowed and they were hard like glacial ice. There was a lethal calmness in his expression.

Hank whistled. 'And what do we do? They could be anywhere by now.'

Alex slapped the paper against his open palm. 'They say they'll be in touch to tell us what they want. We have a first-class sonar system. We'll fix the position of every ship between here and the mainland, and within sailing distance. They may be out of sight, but they spied on us, came here, grabbed the girls and took them back to their ship quite easily. A big ship is loud, so they must have used a smaller boat to reach us. Somehow I don't think they're very far away.'

'There are dozens of ships in this area.'

'True, but we'll start with the ones in the direct vicinity. We can listen in to wireless messages, or anything else that gives us a clue to who they are. I think the one we're looking for will keep quiet, not wanting to give itself away. We'll eliminate them, one by one. I'll start checking straight away. Is Gary still down in the engine room?'

Hank nodded. 'I think he said he was topping up on the oil.'

The smouldering expression and his chilled eyes mirrored Alex's mood. 'Tell him what's happened and that we might need to move out at any time.' He frowned, his anger growing. 'Billy, come with me! We need to get things moving.' He looked around. 'We were just metres away in our cabins, and we didn't notice a thing! If anything happens to them, I'll never forgive myself, and I don't think any of you will either.'

Billy put his hand on his shoulder. 'Whoever's behind it waited until we were asleep, so that means they didn't come on board until the early hours of this morning. It's not eight o'clock yet, so they only have a couple of hours' head start. Like you said, they wouldn't bring their parent ship too close to ours because of the noise. If they used a dingy for the last bit we can calculate the furthest distance the parent ship might be. I bet my bottom dollar their parent ship is still anchored in the same position they started from. They think we won't be able to figure out where they are.'

'Then they're wrong, because we will. Let's get started.'

Billy said, 'I'm with you all the way, but we ought to inform the police. If we don't and it backfires, we'll end up in prison ourselves. Explain what's happened and that we're going to start to search for them. Whose waters are we in at present?'

Hank nodded silently and then said,

'Billy has a point there.'

Anger was still written on his face, but Alex nodded. 'Okay. I'm not sure. It'll depend on how close we are to the nearest island and which country owns it.'

'Well let's sort that out and get in touch with their police. What about getting in touch with Maria's father as well? Do you know where Zoe comes from?'

'I'll get in touch and warn him. I know nothing about Zoe. If it comes to the crunch, I'll have to contact her boss for details. I'll wait until we know more before I contact anyone. I hope to God I won't need to.'

15

Zoe slumped onto the grubby-looking bunk bed and said, 'What can we do?'

Maria shrugged. 'Wait, I suppose. I get the impression that they seem to think Alex will agree to whatever they demand.'

'Somehow I don't think Alex will. He's too determined and stubborn.'

'Agreed, but he's good at judging a situation and when he has to give way. He won't take unnecessary risks, I'm sure about that. Our hands are tied, no matter what he decides to do. Not literally anymore, thank heavens — but we can't do much, can we?'

Frustrated, Zoe muttered, 'There must be something!'

Maria threw back her black hair and laughed. 'Oh, Zoe! What? We're shut up in a cabin on a ship we haven't seen by daylight. We have no idea of the ship's framework, where anything is. Outside that door there are at least three, four, or possibly more men. They intend to keep us here until they get what they want. Alex doesn't know where we are and I can't begin to guess either. We were travelling in that inflatable for a while, so this ship is not within Alex's sight. Where do they start looking? We could be anywhere.'

Zoe got up and gave the cabin and the adjoining bathroom a quick inspection. 'Bah! This place is so grimy and dirty. There's a towel in there that looks like they've been using it as a floor cloth. There is a foul-looking nailbrush, and some washing soap. I need to do something. I'm going to scrub that towel and hang it out of the porthole to dry. I'm scared to lift the lid of the toilet because of what I'll find. I don't know who lived in here before, but it certainly wasn't Mr. Proper. Let's do something, Maria. We need to distract ourselves.'

Maria nodded and they set about

stripping the grimy beds and stacking things out of the way in one of the corners. It was hot in the cabin and it got hotter as time went on. The towel dried quickly in the breeze as it hung from the open porthole.

After a while, the lock in the door rattled and they waited expectantly. One man waited outside again while another came in with a pack of six large water bottles under his arm and a bowl with something that looked liked stew. He eyed them warily, dumped the things and left quickly. There was only one bowl and one spoon.

'Thank heavens for the water. I think we'd die if we drank the stuff that's coming out of the taps in the bathroom.' Maria advanced on the bowl and picked up the spoon. She tried some on the tip of the spoon. Making a face, she said, 'It tastes awful. I'm sorry for them if that's what they're eating. Let's hope they don't figure out that you can cook, or they'll chain you day and night to the stove in the galley!'

Zoe had to laugh. 'I'm not hungry. We can ask them for some bread or something more solid next time someone comes; perhaps they'll go along with the request.' She looked at the messy mix in the bowl. 'I don't like the look of that either. I don't even want to try it. At least it shows us that they don't intend to let us die. They need us to negotiate.'

Maria's expression grew darker. 'Do you realize that eliminating us is a real possibility? If Alex can't find us, or if he refuses to negotiate, no one will ever find us. They only need to throw us overboard to get rid of us permanently.' She wrapped her arms around herself and looked tearful.

Zoe didn't want to admit how much the idea frightened her. She couldn't bear the thought of never seeing her family, friends, or Alex again. She imagined her parents' agony if they didn't know what had happened to her. Gripping Maria by the shoulders, she said, 'Stop it! Think positively. We have to find a way of signalling we're here, in case Alex starts searching the area. There must be something we can use, no matter how small.'

Maria brushed her hand across her cheeks and straightened. 'Yes, you're right. Any ideas?'

Zoe pondered and looked towards the open porthole. It was the only means of cooling the air in the cabin. It was much too small to use as an escape route, and that was why the leader of the gang didn't object to opening it. 'What about . . . ' She searched around. ' . . . a colourful bit of material? Normally, no one hangs anything from a porthole. I know we've dried the towel by hanging it outside already, but no one does that usually.' Zoe picked up the handkerchiefs the men had tied round their mouths. One was quite large and had a bright red pattern; the other was a little smaller in dark blue and white. 'We could tie these two together. We need something else to tie them to the hinge, then they can flutter in the wind. Someone might see it.'

Maria looked sceptical but nodded. 'Okay.'

'Someone could see a towel from on deck, but I doubt if they will spot a small handkerchief from up there.'

'Yes, and anyone searching for us will have trouble seeing it too, for the same reason.'

Exasperated, Zoe said, 'I expect so, but I'm sure they are searching for us. They'll use binoculars, won't they? These hankies will signal where we are.'

'You mean, that's if they find us in the first place.'

'I wish you'd stop being so pessimistic all the time. Just sitting around on our backsides and moaning about the situation won't get us anywhere, will it?' Zoe grabbed the two handkerchiefs and knotted them firmly together with the red one on the end. She looked around for something to fix it to the open porthole.

Maria sheepishly removed the cord that tightened the waistband of her pants and handed it to Zoe.

Zoe took it, gave her a tentative hug and smiled. 'Thanks. It's just the thing.'

Tying their signal to the hinge only took a minute, and once it was in place they stood further away to decide if anyone would be able to notice it. The cord was a light grey colour and it would catch the eye of even the most stupid criminal. Maria suggested rubbing it across the floor until it was really dirty. When they re-attached it a second time, it was no longer so noticeable.

'There!' Satisfied, Zoe stood on a chair and peeked out of the porthole and down at their signal waving in the wind. She jumped down and put the chair back in a corner. 'Unless one of the men hangs right over the railings right above us, they won't see it.'

★   ★   ★

No one else came to check on them for the rest of the day. It was still warm in the cabin when daylight began to fade.

For some reason, the men had already removed the lighting from the ceiling in main cabin, or it had never functioned. A faint light from the bathroom was their only source of lighting. Zoe climbed onto the top bunk and folded her arms behind her head on the grubby mattress.

Maria moved uneasily down below. 'Do you think they're looking?'

Sounding more confident than she felt, Zoe said, 'Of course they are! We just have to be patient.'

Neither of them could sleep. Sometime after dark, Zoe thought she heard something foreign-sounding among the usual creaks and groans of the old ship floating on the surface of the waves. She sat up quickly, nearly banging her head on the ceiling and listened more carefully. Was it just her imagination? Then she heard the pinging sound again. Jumping down, she went to the porthole. On the way, she trod on something. Picking it up, she looked at it in the faint light. It looked like a dried pea.

Maria swung her legs over the edge of her bunk and whispered, 'What's wrong? What's up?'

'I don't know. I heard something.' Zoe got a chair, stood on it and sneaked a quick look, grasping the edges of the porthole.

In the darkness somewhere below, coming from amid the lapping of the waves against the ship, a familiar voice called quietly, 'Are you all right? Are they treating you okay?'

It was Alex! She smothered the feeling of sheer relief to reply, 'Yes, we're both fine.'

'Good. How many men are there?'

'We don't know. We've seen four, but there could be more.'

'Can you see me?'

'No.'

His voice was hushed. 'Okay! I'll swim further back and hope you can see me then. Wave if you do. We're planning to get you out of there, so be prepared at any time.'

'Yes.' Zoe heard the sound of

movement in the water and examined the area limited to her sight. Suddenly she saw Alex treading water and her spirits rose. She waved her hand to show him she'd seen him, and then beckoned to Maria. Jumping down, Zoe said, 'He's over to the left. It's not easy to see him, but once you've adjusted to the movement of the waves, you'll be able to pick him out okay. You're probably better at it than me.'

Maria scrambled up into place and tilted her head to look for him. After a minute or so, she was successful and stuck her hand out of the porthole to wave. She remained in place and watched. 'He just waved back and disappeared.' Climbing down and moving the chair back to the side, she continued, 'They know where we are, and that means they're planning to rescue us. I wish he'd told us what they're planning.'

'Voices are easily heard at night because everything else is quiet. Someone on board might have heard him going into details. He just wanted to reassure us, and he did. I wonder where the *Astrea* is. Not within sight of this ship, otherwise our hosts would be at panic stations. We've been anchored in the same spot since we arrived.'

Maria sounded a lot more cheerful. 'Alex is a great swimmer, one of the best. I expect when they figured out where we might be, they used the dinghy to come closer, and he swam the last bit. How did you notice he was there?'

Zoe shrugged. 'I just heard something. I also found this on the floor.' She showed her the dried pea. 'I presume Alex threw it through the porthole. No easy task in a moving sea. I wonder how he kept it dry.'

'Oh, diving suits have watertight pockets. I expect he had them with him deliberately. I feel so much better now, don't you?'

'Of course. If we had a bottle of champagne I think I'd get drunk.'

Maria laughed. 'I'd join you. At least we know they've found us. We ought to get some sleep. We might need to be in top form tomorrow.'

Zoe thought that wouldn't be easy, and it wasn't. She lay on her bunk in the muggy atmosphere of the small cabin and hoped that Alex and the others had a good plan. Daylight was breaking when she finally fell asleep.

16

'Alex? Is she all right?'

'She seems to be fine.'

'You've seen her?'

'The two women are okay; they waved. They know we'll try to free them as fast as possible.'

'You spoke to Maria?'

'Not directly. I spoke a few words with the other woman. I asked if they were all right and she said yes.'

'Why didn't you talk to Maria?'

'Hernandez, it was too dangerous to talk to anyone. I wanted to make sure the women were okay before we made final plans. I was there in the middle of the night, but these crooks might have seen me or heard me. I didn't stay long.'

The radio connection crackled. 'And what are you going to do now?'

'I've alerted the police and they're

sending a patrol. They weren't even certain themselves who's responsible for these waters and were checking first. Apparently, we're between two nautical authorities. They'll send a launch as soon as possible. It will take ages to get here and we don't intend to hang around waiting. We're planning to board the ship this evening and we're preparing for that now.'

There was approval in Maria's father's voice. 'Yes, do that. I know you'll do your best. I trust you, whatever happens. I thought that if she came on your expedition she was safe, but it seems she's not safe anywhere.'

Staring out of the window with the microphone in his hand, Alex said, 'It's not just Maria I'm worried about; there's the other woman as well. She has nothing to do with our search or Maria's dilemma, but she's been dragged into it anyway. She's probably in more danger, because she wasn't part of their plans. They won't hesitate to get rid of her if she gets in the way.'

'Get them out, Alex. We won't have a moment's peace until we know they're safe again.'

'I realize that, and I'll let you know as soon as we've got them, I promise.'

'Good luck! I wish I could help. Do your best; I can't ask for more.'

'I will. Bye, Hernandez.'

★   ★   ★

Alex called a meeting on the bridge. 'You all know how things stand. I agreed to bring Maria along and she's my responsibility. Indirectly Zoe is too, because I involved her unnecessarily. There's no guarantee that one of us won't get hurt. There are at least four men on that ship, conceivably more. We don't know its exact layout, although I can make a rough guess because I've seen similar ships before. I think it's an old coastal transporter. I didn't see anyone patrolling or keeping watch last night, but I couldn't see the deck clearly from the water. I know now that the two girls are in a cabin in the bow of the ship, starboard side. I'm hoping the element of surprise will give us the advantage we need to overrun them. If there are more men than estimated it could be messy, and I'm hoping that you'll help but I'll understand if you opt out. This was meant to be a treasure hunt, not a rescue undertaking.'

Hank uttered grimly, 'We're with you, all of us. All the way. Wait till we get our hands on them.'

Alex grinned softly. 'I think it's best to use the outboard to get in as close as possible again like last time, and use oars for the final bit. We'll have to guess when we are still out of earshot or not. When we reach that point I'll go overboard, get on deck, and check if they have a lookout. Once I know the coast is clear, I'll give you a signal and then you come alongside and join me. I hope we can get that far without anyone noticing. On board, we split up. Billy and Gary, you two make for the bridge and tackle anyone wandering on deck. Hank and I will go below deck straight away and try to locate the women's cabin. Hopefully we won't meet any opposition on the way. Our paramount objective is to find the women and get out of there fast. No one should act the hero. If we can get them out without a fight, all the better. If not . . . '

Gary intervened. 'But they shouldn't get away scot-free!'

'I agree, but let's get the women out of there before we worry about grabbing them for the police. If the police arrive on time, we'll leave it up to them to handle the punishment side of things. It's up to the police to go on board and arrest them. We don't have to do their job. I'm only interested in freeing the women. If these people see us before we find the girls there's bound to be a struggle of some kind. Once the police get involved, there's also a danger of a shooting match because they'll get more desperate. Our main aim should be to get Maria and

Zoe out uninjured. If the police were around from the word go, these crooks would feel manoeuvred into a corner, and use the women as human shields.'

Billy nodded. 'Yes, you're right. Let's hope for the best.'

Alex straightened and eyed them all determinedly. 'We don't have any guns on board, but we do have a couple of harpoons. We'll take them with us and use them if necessary. I'm sure the police will be hopping mad when they arrive and find we didn't wait. Normally I would wait for the police but we don't know how long they'll stay put. The harpoons are our only means of defending ourselves. If it's necessary we'll use them.'

Hank said, 'I'll look around and see if we can use something as clubs too.'

'Okay, let's use the rest of the time to check and prepare.'

17

After they'd seen Alex in the water, Zoe and Maria chatted for a while and eventually fell asleep. When they woke, they knew that the coming day would stretch endlessly. There wouldn't be any action during daylight hours.

The tramp of approaching feet announced the return of at least one of their hijackers. The women moved away from the door and waited until it opened. One of the men had some more water and what looked like a packet of biscuits and some green bananas.

He grinned. 'Here you are, my lovelies — something to keep you going. We're expecting our friend to get in touch today. We'll soon know one way or the other.'

Maria spitted poison in his direction. 'When we get out of here you'll get the punishment you deserve. What makes you think you can get away with it?'

He grinned. 'Because that's all part of the plan. We know what we're doing.' He peered at her more intently through his narrow dark eyes and laughed. 'Missing your boyfriend, are you, Maria? There's no need for that. There are men here, real men, who are willing to console you any time. I'm one of them, for a start.' He reached out to her and threw his arm around her, pulling her close.

Maria stared at him with incensed eyes. She tried to push him away. 'Take your dirty hands off me, you pig.'

His features hardened and then he chuckled nastily as he bent his head to kiss her. Maria pushed him away harder and he laughed.

Zoe was frightened and her stomach was knotted, but she grabbed the chair and brought it down over his head. He stumbled and let go of Maria. He grabbed the framework of the door and the racket alarmed someone else. The Mexican came running, came inside, and took in the situation at a glance. Grabbing the man in the room by his collar, he threw him head first out into the corridor and shouted at him. 'Are you loco? Do you know what'll happen to us if we don't keep the agreement, and you cause trouble?' Looking at the chair on the floor, he kicked it aside. Making a sweeping gesture with his hand, he said, 'My apologies. He forgot himself. I'll make sure nothing like that happens again.'

Too angry to react otherwise, Zoe shouted at him, 'You better had!' She added, 'If anyone tries that again, they'll be sorry.' It was an empty threat, but they shouldn't think they were afraid of them.

The yellow teeth grinned at her outburst. 'Tut, tut! And I always thought women were supposed to be the gentle sex. I can see why our client is so enamoured. You're a pair of firebrands, aren't you?'

Maria uttered, 'What do you mean, 'our client'?'

He didn't answer but turned on his heel and slammed the door behind him. The key turned in the lock.

Zoe sat down on the bunk and pulled Maria next to her. 'Are you all right? That was horrible. I thought for a minute he might . . . '

'Yes, so did I. Thanks for your attack with the chair.' She laughed weakly. 'You're not a quiet, docile little lamb after all, are you?'

'Sheer reaction.' Zoe straightened up again and lodged the remains of the chair against the door. 'We didn't see any of them all day yesterday, so I presume that won't happen today either. I just hope that Alex and the others will come soon. I won't move that chair again until I hear a familiar voice.'

Maria viewed the chair sceptically. 'It isn't much of an obstacle, but it's better than nothing. It's going to be a long day.'

18

The sea was calm and the oars ploughed through the water. The dinghy sped across the choppy waves and the men on board were silent and focused on the ship ahead of them. There was no sign of movement on deck, although the nautical lights were correctly in place. They were approaching the port side and saw the red light in the darkness. They knew that the ship hadn't changed its location for the last two days. The sonar equipment had helped them eliminate the unlikely ships in the area and conclude this ship was where they'd find the girls. They'd calculated the distance and Alex had successfully made contact the previous night.

Now Alex slipped over the side when they were a hundred meters away. The others anchored the boat and prepared to join him as soon as he gave them a signal. Alex swam underwater. He was a silent dark figure unnoticed by anyone checking from deck level. Staring through the darkness, the other three men waiting in the dinghy followed his progress and spoke in hushed tones.

Reaching the hull, Alex surfaced. Waiting for the swell of the water to help him, he reached up and grabbed the bottom rung of the rope ladder and started to climb. Almost on eye-level with the deck, he checked his immediate surroundings and found it was clear. He came on board and silently removed his air-tank, stacking it out of sight nearby. He moved across the deck stealthily, using the shadows to cover his movements. There was light burning on the bridge, but he couldn't detect any movement. If the ship was securely anchored, it wasn't likely that anyone would be stationed there permanently. An occasional instrument check would suffice.

A few minutes later, he'd rounded

the deck and met no one. Back at his starting point, he extracted a small, powerful torch from a pocket and gave the signal the men in the dinghy were waiting for. Before long he heard the dinghy below and his crew climbing the rope ladder. Within minutes, they were all assembled on deck.

Alex whispered, 'The only place on deck where there could be someone is the bridge, so I think one of us can cover that. Gary, if you take care of that, the rest of us will go below deck. If you find no one on the bridge, you can join us below.'

Gary nodded. 'Right!'

'The rest of you, follow me.'

A few minutes later all hell broke loose when Alex and the others began to bang on cabin doors along the gangway where Alex figured the women must be. They reckoned that the noise was bound to wake the crooks too, but speed and surprise were their object. Some of the kidnappers tumbled half-asleep out of cabins further down the gangway. Alex counted five of them. They halted their rush when they spotted Hank and Billy aiming harpoons at them. The Mexican gave Alex and the others a sickening smile.

Maria and Zoe heard the rumpus, hammered on their cabin door, and called out.

The Mexican uttered through thin lips, 'How do you expect to get out of here in one piece? You have to pass us to get back on deck and that won't be easy, my friend.'

Alex moved a few steps back to the door where the women were shouting. He looked down and commented, 'How convenient, you've left the key outside.' He turned it deftly, and without waiting to check on the women, he concentrated on the opponents again. The Mexican was clearly the leader. 'Perhaps you won't laugh when the police get here. They're on their way. Kidnapping carries a death sentence in some places. At the very minimum, a long prison sentence.'

The Mexican grinned. 'They have to catch us first, *amigo*!'

'You did this just because of the treasure?'

The man looked confused. 'Treasure? What treasure? Maria's husband got lonely and wanted to see her again. He's willing to pay us a tidy sum if we collect her from your ship and hand her over. We're waiting for money and further instructions.'

Now it was Alex's turn to look confused and surprised. 'You're after Maria? Her ex-husband organized all this? He's under a court order not to come within five miles of wherever she is. Did you know that?'

'No, but what does that matter? He wanted us to hang on to her until he'd arranged for the money to pay us, and then we'll dump her wherever he suggested. The other woman just got in the way. We didn't expect to find anyone else in that cabin. She would have given the alarm so we had to take her. We intended to dump her too. This whole job is turning into a nightmare.'

Without further comment, Alex nodded to the other two and they moved a step forward. Hank and Billy lifted their harpoons. Alex said, 'I'm giving you the chance to get out of the way. Two of you will get harpooned if you stay, and there's another man on deck who'll join us in a few minutes. Then the odds will be level, and you also have the police on your tails too. Save your skins!'

One of the men shouted excitedly in Spanish to the Mexican and the others joined in loudly. Soon they all scuttled away to hurry upstairs. The Mexican gave Alex and the others a final hostile look, turned on his heel and dashed after them.

Alex watched for a moment before he hammered on the door. 'Maria, Zoe, it's safe to come out now. Hurry up. We've got to get off this ship fast.'

The women opened the door and Maria fell sobbing into Alex's arms. Right behind her, Zoe looked away and sidled past them. Billy was standing directly behind Alex and she gave Billy a tremulous smile. 'Are we glad to see you.'

Billy threw his arm around her shoulder and gave her a tight hug. 'And are we glad to see you! Come on, let's get off this tub before they start the engine. Gary's on deck somewhere.'

Zoe said, 'I'm ready. Let's go.'

Maria calmed down at last and detached herself from Alex's arms. Billy, Hank and Zoe made their way cautiously along the passageway and Alex and Maria made up the rear.

Gary was waiting expectantly at the head of the rope ladder. 'I was listening to the rumpus and was about to join you when I noticed my help wasn't needed; I saw the men scuttling for the bridge. They're making preparations to up anchor. Our dinghy is ready and waiting.'

Billy clapped him on the shoulder. 'Then we need to move fast.' He turned to Zoe. 'Gary goes first and then you follow, all right?'

Zoe nodded. She felt too numbed by the happenings and the picture of Maria in Alex's arms to do anything else.

Once they were in the dinghy and on their way back to Alex's ship, they looked back at the other ship with its handful of navigation lights. They heard the cranking of the anchors, and the ship moved off slowly into the darkness to the steady beat of its engines. Clearly, the threat of police intervention was stronger than the desire to fight. They needed to get away fast.

They were nearly all feeling euphoric that things had gone so well, and the men spoke excitedly among themselves. Zoe and Maria huddled together, seated on a narrow central bench. Zoe couldn't feel malicious about Maria and Alex. Why should she? Maria and she had shared a few harrowing days and they were now tentative friends. After a few minutes, Alex called Maria and she went to him, keeping her balance easily on the moving boat. They had a whispered conversation. Zoe felt very alone and very superfluous.

Billy handed Zoe his thick sweater and the extra warmth was more than welcome. She wasn't certain if she was cold because of shock of the rescue, because of the cool air zipping across her skin, or because of the memory of Maria in Alex's arms. Alex hadn't spoken directly to her since their release and he now had his arm round Maria's shoulders again as they were talking. Zoe tried to ignore them. Whatever he was telling her, it looked like Maria didn't like what she heard and needed his comfort.

Zoe forced herself to look out across the dark water. It hurt her to see how much they meant to each other and she tried hard to control an all-consuming disappointment. She had to leave. She didn't know how yet, but there had to be a way.

She couldn't stay. She was in love with Alex. It had happened despite all her efforts to ignore him. There was a lot about Alex Harding she didn't understand and couldn't wholly accept, but it made no difference: she loved him. Her problem was that she couldn't contemplate love without loyalty and devotion, and it looked like those were already given elsewhere.

The journey back to the *Astrea* didn't take long, and once Zoe was on board she used the excuse of needing a shower so that she could disappear fast to let her tears mix freely with the water flowing over her body. Feeling better able to cope, she went on deck and met Maria.

'Thanks for being a friend during the last two days,' Maria said. 'I'm so glad you were with me. I think I'd have gone crazy if I'd been on my own.'

Zoe smiled. She couldn't dislike her, even though she was getting Alex. In the beginning she'd thought Maria was high and mighty, but she now realized that she was as susceptible as any other woman. 'I'm glad we were together. You're strong and I'm sure you would have managed very well without me. It was something neither of us will ever forget.' Zoe gave her a quick hug. 'I'm going to make myself a sandwich and then I'm going to bed.'

Maria nodded and smiled. 'Good idea. I'm going to have a shower and then I've promised to share a beer with the others. Join us?'

Zoe shook her head and smiled. 'I need to unwind.' In the galley Zoe made herself some sandwiches, then took them outside to eat in a quiet spot on deck. After two days without real food, they tasted wonderful. Billy found her there.

'How do you feel?'

Zoe looked up at him. 'I'm fine. It's great to know we're safe again. Thanks to you and all the others.'

He brushed her thanks aside and shifted his weight. 'I'm glad no one got injured. It looks like you just happened to be in the wrong place at the wrong time. I think they only reckoned with finding Maria. When they found you as well, they decided on the spur of the moment it was easier to take you along.'

She nodded. 'What's happening now? Are the police on the way?'

'Yeah. Alex has been in touch, given them our position and where we found them. He told them what happened. They weren't pleased that we went ahead without them. Alex thinks the crooks are heading into another section of international waters, to make things more complicated. They must know their way around this area very well. The police may not then have the power to intervene and will need to involve another police force. They still need signed statements and will have to get any descriptions we can give them. So we have to wait and see if they're initially too busy chasing the crooks or if they pass it on to colleagues in another patch of the Caribbean and come here for statements.'

'I was just going to bed. I feel ready to drop.' It wasn't the truth, but she had to avoid everyone for a while.

'Then go. The police won't turn up for a while yet, and by the time they've finished with the rest of us you'll be feeling a lot fresher.'

Zoe reached up and gave his cheek a quick peck. 'Thanks!' She left him, left her plate in the sink and went below. Maria had showered and was on her way upstairs again. 'Change your mind? Coming?'

Zoe shook her head. 'I'm tired. Enjoy yourself.'

Maria nodded and left.

Lying on her camp bed staring into the dark, dozens of thoughts whizzed through Zoe's brain. Ever since she'd met Alex Harding, everything in her life had changed with a bang. She thought back over the last weeks and the few special moments they'd shared. She thought about Billy and what he said about the police. She sat up and wrapped her arms around her knees. That was her way out. Somehow, she'd persuade them to take her back when they went.

19

Zoe felt better when dawn finally arrived, even though she hadn't slept very much. Maria was already awake and gone. She stuffed her belongings and cosmetic bag into her holdall. She could see there was a police cruiser tied up alongside, though hadn't heard it arrive, and she was glad to see it. Voices came from near the bow of the ship. Zoe went to the galley first to get herself some coffee. She wasn't hungry.

Taking her mug with her, she went to a quiet corner and leaned against the railings. The fresh breezes brushed her face and despite everything, she couldn't help loving the start of another day in paradise. She was still deep in thought when she noticed Alex had joined her. Her heart thumped painfully with love, but an unwelcome tension loomed and grew between them because they were both silent.

Finally, he said, 'I'm sorry I didn't have time to ask if you were okay yesterday. There was so much going on and too much chaos for a while.'

Her breath caught in her throat, but she managed to look at him and reply, 'That's all right, I realized that. Don't worry about it. I'm just grateful that you found us.' She looked out across the water. 'The police are here?'

He leaned on the railings. The tantalizing smell of his aftershave wafted across to her. 'Yes, they've been interviewing everyone. I expect they'll want to see you too.'

She nodded and gripped the rail tightly. 'How's Maria this morning? I haven't seen her.'

'From what I gather, she's okay and back to her normal self.'

'Good.'

'And you?'

'Me? I'm fine.' She tried a reassuring smile, but it didn't work.

'You don't look fine. You have dark shadows under your eyes.'

With a weak smile, she uttered, 'Those are just the kind of encouraging words I need to make me feel better.'

He ran his hand down his face. 'I didn't mean it in that way and you know it. I'm just trying to say I'm worried about you.'

Trying to sound cheerful, Zoe said, 'Don't worry. Being shut up on board ship for two days with a bunch of idiotic kidnappers is not going to dent my stiff upper lip. Isn't that what the English are supposed to get when they face an adversary?'

He laughed softly. 'So they say. If that's true, it must be something in the genes, and we only realize what could have gone wrong later when it's all over.'

'Then perhaps Maria's approach is better. I'm okay, honestly. I don't feel panicky now, and I'm very grateful that you all took a risk and rescued us. I don't intend to think about what happened more than I have to. I'm hoping it'll fade from my memory and end up as an exciting incident to tell my grandchildren one day, if I ever have any.'

His expression was unreadable and his pale grey eyes stared at the lights dancing on the aquamarine waters.

He was what she'd coveted all her life, but he wasn't for her. She felt a terrible sense of loss as she started to turn away from him. It wasn't sensible to stay here with him. She was almost looking forward to going ashore. She stopped functioning for a moment when he reached out and ran his hand down her face. The feel of his fingers brushing her cheek gave her the wildest urge to jump back. He was danger with a big D. Just his touch wakened longings she'd never known before. She had the feeling that if she'd given him the kind of indication he wanted at that moment, she'd have landed up in his arms again.

She didn't. Instead, she decided to be

honest and stop fooling around with her own emotions. She found enough courage to say, 'Please, let's stay just friends. I don't want to complicate my life with the wrong kind of involvement. We don't match. You're someone who thinks flirting, or sex, is more important than commitment. You worry more about scoring than dating, and you feel rewarded when you make it with lots of women. You probably believe marriage is, at best, a long-term benefit of some kind, while sex is an immediate and permanent preoccupation. Maria is devoted to you. Be content with that. I'm too old-fashioned for you. We don't fit.'

He stiffened. His expression bordered on mockery as he straightened. 'I'd like to know exactly what you mean, because I think you're only afraid to follow your instincts. You can't deny there's something between us. Why aren't you willing to give it a try? Who knows where it'll lead.'

Alarm mixed with anger rippled

along her spine. 'I just tried to explain why. Because you are you. How many girls have you left along the way, Alex? I simply don't want to be another one. You have Maria; be contented with that. I don't need that kind of hassle in my life.' He opened his mouth to say something but she ploughed on, giving him no chance. 'I'm not audacious enough to play around just for fun. That's not my style.'

'You mean it, don't you? I can understand your reactions but I'm asking you to give me, to give us, a chance. You don't know the whole truth.'

Zoe noticed Gary coming towards them. She shook her head. 'I can't.' She was glad when he called out.

'Alex! The inspector wants a word with you.'

Glowering first at Gary, and then at her, Alex muttered, 'Damn it!' He turned away without another word and followed Gary towards the bridge.

Zoe was glad he hadn't noticed how

her hands were shaking, or that her expression now showed how desperately she wished she had enough courage to throw caution to the wind.

20

By the time the police eventually asked to see her, she had a splitting headache but she knew the interview would be the only chance she had of getting away from Alex fast. She had to persuade them to take her as a passenger.

They were friendly and professional. They asked her about how she was taken prisoner and for details about the time they were shut up in the cabin, as well as for descriptions of any of the men. Taking down information from her passport, one of them said, 'I expect you'll be glad to go home and see friends and family again after what's happened, since you were only on board by chance and aren't an official member of the team.'

'That's very true. I only intended to stay on board until the next time they needed new supplies. Now I'm more than ready to leave because of what's happened. In fact, I wondered if you could do me a huge favour and take me back to the mainland with you. I'm sure you'll understand that after what happened here, I'm nervous and anxious to get away as fast as possible.'

He looked sympathetic but said, 'I'm sorry but that's not allowed. We represent the authorities. We're not here to provide transportation for the general public. If our superiors found out we'd done so, we'd be in trouble.'

Zoe pleaded, 'If you'd caught some of those men, you'd have taken them into custody and then back with you, wouldn't you?'

'Yes, but that's different. We have to get potential criminals behind bars as soon as possible, even when we arrest them at sea. They aren't passengers in the sense you mean.'

'Please! I promise I won't get in your way. And I'll leave the ship discreetly as soon as you reach the mainland. I'll make my way to the nearest airport from there and head for home. If I stay here, I'll just go on thinking about what happened. I won't be able to sleep, and I'm sure I'll end up having nightmares.'

The policeman was momentarily silent, then he got up and went across the room to speak quietly to his colleague. Zoe could see the second man shrug his shoulders. When he returned to her, he had a slight smile on his face. 'Okay, I've talked to my friend and he says it's all right, as long as you promise never to mention how you got back. If you did, we'll end up in hot water.'

Delighted, some of the tension faded and Zoe replied, 'I won't, I promise. Thank you so much. When are you intending to leave?'

'Soon. In fact if you're coming with us, as soon as you're ready. We've finished taking statements and there's nothing else we can do here anymore. Our colleagues controlling the next international stretch of waters have taken up the hunt. Let's hope they'll catch them before they slip into a port somewhere and sell the boat. At the moment, finding the boat is our best chance of finding them. Once that's changed hands, or disappeared, the group will break up and it will be almost impossible to find them. Perhaps they've already organized a hideaway.'

'It sounds like it's a race against time.'

'It is.' He added with more bitterness in his voice, 'There's a chance they'll escape completely. If they can hide the boat, and make some changes to its appearance, they'll be off the hook. No one saw it by daylight and apart from the description we have from Mr. Harding and the others, no one knows with certainty what it was like — how old, the type of ship, its condition, etcetera.' He shuffled some papers together. 'If you'll get your belongings, we'll leave. Perhaps you'd like to say a brief goodbye to the others first?'

Feeling elated that she'd persuaded them to take her with them, Zoe went to look for the others and explained she was going. They sympathized and said they understood. Hank and Gary gave her a hug and wished her luck.

Billy was pensive. 'I can understand why, but do you think it's a good idea? A couple of relaxing days on board would do you the world of good. We'll have to return to port earlier than we expected now, to top up the oxygen supplies. I promise we'll take better care of you from now on.'

Zoe laughed and reached up to kiss his cheek. 'You always have. What happened was a fluke. I liked being with you all on board. I wasn't even seasick. Did anyone find out what the men were planning to do with us?'

He shrugged. 'Not exactly, but we can guess. We think we know who was behind it too.'

'Really? I hope you told the police. Take care of yourself Billy, and take care of everyone else on the *Astrea*. Good luck with the search, and if you ever come to London, get in touch. We'll go out and live it up a bit.'

He laughed and ruffled her hair. 'You take care of yourself. I hope that we'll see each other again soon. You were a welcome visitor, and we'll miss your cooking like hell!'

'And not a MacDonald's in sight! Shall I send you food parcels?' Zoe suddenly realized she would miss him; miss them all. They'd been friends for a while. She wondered if she'd ever see any of them again.

She found Maria busy checking the air tanks and the gauges. Maria was surprised when Zoe explained she was going, but with a knowing expression she said, 'You don't feel comfortable here anymore, do you?'

Zoe pretended complacency. 'I'm not desperately unhappy. I just want to get back to my old life and my work again.'

Maria stood up and gave her a big hug. 'I understand that. I'll miss you, and the others will too.'

With a lump in her throat, Zoe joked, 'Billy just told me he'll miss my cooking.'

'Billy and I are not the only ones who will miss you, and not just because of your cooking. Are you sure that you want to leave?'

'Yes, I'm determined.'

'Good luck then, and keep in touch.'

Zoe nodded and then went below to fetch her holdall. When she returned Alex was standing next to the policemen. His eyes were icy as he watched her join them. His confident, arrogant appearance as he viewed her unsettled her completely for a moment, but she thrust it aside.

His voice had an undertone of coldness. 'Billy told me that you're leaving.'

She was glad they weren't on their own. She hoped her smile looked genuine. 'Yes, these kind gentlemen have agreed to let me travel back with them. Thanks for everything, Alex.'

He shrugged and she could tell from the expression in his face that he was angry. 'Do what you like if you can't stand it here anymore.' He turned to the policemen and held out his hand. 'Thank you. You'll let us know if there are any new developments?'

'Yes, sir. Of course.'

Alex nodded. He studied Zoe with a thoroughness she didn't like. With barely a noticeable final acknowledgement in her direction, he left, leaving them to board the police cruiser unaided.

It was clear he was angry with her. Why? Just because she'd given him the cold shoulder? Zoe felt a little stunned as the men helped her and her holdall aboard their ship. Alex hadn't even waited to help, and he hadn't offered her a word of kindness in farewell either. She'd done nothing to deserve his anger, but it was clear that he was mad at her. Was it just because she'd told him they didn't match? Why should he care? He still had Maria, and to all intents and purposes it looked like he had plenty of other girlfriends waiting on the sidelines too. He was probably put out because he wasn't used to women turning him down, but she was no loss to someone like him.

As the cruiser drew away from the *Astrea* she waved at Billy, who'd come to the railings to see them off. He took off his baseball cap and waved it until they were out of sight. With tears in her eyes, she stood watching until Alex's ship was a small white spot on the horizon. Brushing her cheeks with the back of her hand, she went to look for a quiet spot to spend the rest of the journey.

21

Zoe had to do some island-hopping to get back to the international airport, but no one was expecting her back in London anyway, so it didn't really matter. She could have stayed and played the tourist — no one in London would be any the wiser — but she didn't want to face being in paradise on her own. She winced when she thought about the mounting air fares and her credit card payments.

During the final flight homeward she had plenty of time to think about Alex and adjust to the new situation. They'd never made it beyond the occasional kiss, but amazingly that was enough for her to know he was the one. It wasn't just the patent physical attraction she felt for him; there was also an invisible emotional level that made him the one man she could imagine spending the rest of her life with. He was intelligent and a clever leader; he had a good sense of humour, and he cared about the people he liked. She loved him; it was as simple as that.

When she reached London, it was a dismal afternoon. She acknowledged that she'd probably never be alone with Alex again, though she might see him with one of the crew if they ever came to the auction. By then she ought to be able to handle it. The knowledge that she'd lost him — although she'd never really had him in the first place — hurt and gnawed her insides, and she wondered how long that would last. She put up with it and hoped that time would heal it. There were sayings about time healing everything, and she hoped they were true.

Concentrating on her job would help. Other hobbies and distractions would absorb her time and energies after work. That was the first logical step. She decided not to tell Lucy how she felt about Alex yet. She never kept secrets from Lucy, but this time it was different. She couldn't share everything until she'd fully adjusted and could talk about him without feeling the loss and the despair.

Next morning, back at work, she knocked briskly and then walked into George's office. He looked over the top of his spectacles. 'Good Lord. I thought you were still sunning yourself.' He smiled and pointed at the visitor's chair. 'Tell me about it and make me envious. I wasn't expecting you back for at least another week. Anyway, that's what William told me.'

'Something unexpected happened. I decided it was time to leave.'

'That sounds interesting. What? Come to think of it, you don't look too good, considering that you've been to the Caribbean.'

Zoe was glad to be back. Her workplace was somewhere she felt confident and in control. She told George about how they'd been taken hostage. He didn't interrupt until she finally explained how she'd returned to the mainland with the police. He whistled softly. 'Good heavens! You read about that sort of thing happening in South America, rucksack-tourists being kidnapped and the like, but I'd never expect it to happen in the Caribbean.'

'I didn't either, but the Caribbean divides North and South America, George. There's no great distance between the two. Perhaps it happens more often than anyone suspects.'

George nodded. 'And why did they do it?'

'I'm not sure, and as far as I know no one else is either. Until the police catch them, no one can be sure about the whys and wherefores. The version I heard was that they were following Alex because they intended to grab the treasure as soon as he'd done the finding.'

George rubbed his chin. His forehead was wrinkled. 'And why did they snatch you and the other woman?'

Zoe shrugged her shoulders. 'Apparently they planned to use us to blackmail Alex into giving it them any treasure on the double.'

He whistled again. 'It sounds like you're lucky to get out unscathed. Did they injure you?'

'They didn't actually terrorize or bully us, except once when one of them tried to grab Maria. We were frightened, but being together helped until Alex and the others arrived to free us. It wasn't a very pleasant experience, and I hope something like that never happens to me again.'

'I bet! Understandably so.'

'George, don't spread it around the company, please. It's over now. If the gutter press gets hold of the story, I might end up on the front page and I'd hate that. The fewer who know about it, the better. I just want to forget it.'

'Yes, of course.' He tilted his head. 'You don't mind me telling my wife, do you? She won't pass it on, I promise. I'll tell her it's a secret.'

Zoe laughed. 'If you must.' She shifted in the chair. 'I'd like an

unpretentious and normal job somewhere within the British Isles, please.
I've had enough excitement for a while.'

'I haven't anything interesting at the
moment. The only task that's open and
no one else wants to take on is one
that's situated somewhere in the depths
of the Highlands. Apparently, the place
is miles from everywhere. The next pub
seems to be fifty miles away and the
house is situated between bogs and
heather-covered hills. The winds blow
at sixty miles an hour, and if temperatures are above freezing for longer than
a couple of days they think it's high
summer.'

She grinned and felt glad to be back.
'I'll take it. It sounds interesting.'

'Really? It's the usual house contents
estimation. The last owner died recently
and the man's heirs want to know
whether it's worth putting the contents
up for auction, or if it would be better
just to make a big bonfire of everything,
before finding some unsuspecting soul
who thinks the place is the perfect

romantic spot for their summer holidays.'

'Travel expenses?' He nodded. 'How long do I have?'

George leaned forward. 'Look, Zoe, I'd be pleased if you did it — delighted, in fact — but are you sure? You've just had a harrowing experience. Are you okay? You're not just running from hidden devils, are you? I don't want to be the one who pushes you over the edge. There's always plenty to do in the office, you know that.'

Zoe ran her fingers through her hair. 'I'm fine, honestly. In fact, I think a couple of days in the peace and quiet of the Scottish hills would be better for me than staying in London at the moment.'

'Well, think about it carefully. If you want to change your mind, I'll understand. If you're still game, I'll dig out all the details and get in touch with the housekeeper to warn her someone is coming.'

'I won't change my mind. When do you want me to leave?'

'The end of this week? I don't have a clue how long you'll need to get the work done. It could take you a day or two, or a week. It all depends on what you find and how much. Just keep in touch.'

She nodded. 'I will. Anything else? How is business generally?'

'Ticking over for a change. William keeps asking if I've heard anything from you or from Alex Harding. Did Alex tell you he'll keep us up to date on progress?'

She looked out of the window for a second. 'I don't honestly know, George. I forgot to ask him when I left. After the police agreed to take me back with them, it went so fast, it just slipped my mind. If he does get in touch with me in the office, someone else can direct his email or phone call to you, can't they? He may even get directly in touch with William. He's spoken to him a couple of times already, so that's more likely, I should think.'

'Was everything going according to

plan when you left?'

'I think so. They'd almost reached the search area when those men kidnapped us, so they must be there by now. They were all set to start searching the seabed. The equipment and everything had been checked and rechecked, and they were ready for action.'

'How long do they need?'

'Haven't a clue. No one ever talked about that. I'm sure that once they get there they won't give up easily. Alex is determined. He's also confident that they are going to find something. The others would follow him to hell and back.' She got up. 'I'll check through my emails now to see if there's anything important.'

'Okay. And I'll sort that Scottish deal out this morning. I'll let you know as soon as I've fixed everything. If you go, don't forget to pack your winter woollies.'

Zoe laughed. 'I won't.' On her way to the door, she looked back at him and said, 'I'm glad to be back, George. I've missed you and I've missed this place.'

Zoe phoned Lucy that evening and told her about how she and Maria had been taken hostage. She could hear the shock in Lucy's voice and reaction. It sounded fantastic even to her own ears. They agreed to meet up at the first opportunity as soon as Zoe got back from Scotland.

The week flashed by. Once she was in Scotland, she was very busy itemizing anything of interest during the day. In the evening she spent her time with the housekeeper. Mrs McDonald was glad to have some company, as the only other permanent employee was a gardener/ chauffeur who lived with his family in a converted flat over the stable buildings. Mrs McDonald kept plying Zoe with food because she was sure that a 'wee lassie' like her needed building up. It was very soothing to sit in the warm kitchen with Mrs. McDonald, who was knitting an item for one of her grand-children. The older woman kept up a flow of conversation about her family as well as the deceased laird's, and Zoe only revealed as much about herself as she wanted to.

Sometimes in the afternoons, after she'd been cataloguing things in the slightly musty rooms for too long, she went for a walk up one of the nearby hills. With the wind whistling past her head and studying the beauty of the Highlands around her, she began to understand why the family had built their home in such a remote spot centuries ago. They were the moments when she allowed herself to think about Alex and wonder what he was doing. She deliberately tried to stop thinking about him but wasn't always successful. Even after reading in bed until she was exhausted and eventually fell asleep, she still dreamt about him. She couldn't shake off all the memories. She told herself it would get better in time.

Zoe was sorry to leave Mrs. McDonald at the end of the week; she was a gem. She reminded Zoe a little of her own mother. She stopped when she reached the crest of hill and the road leading down to the old house to take a last picture for her photo album.

★ ★ ★

On Monday morning she went straight to George's office. He looked up at her from where he was seated, behind his untidy desk. 'Zoe! And — ? Did you get it all down on paper? You look a bit better today. The tan has faded, but so have the shadows under your eyes.'

Zoe lifted her iPad and ignored his last comment. 'It's all here. I have hundreds and hundreds of photos. I haven't made too many guesses about pricing, only the items that I recognize and know about. Do you want me to print the contents out, or just send the appropriate pictures to our various specialists?'

'Email them to our people here in the company and tell them they should comment and estimate. Some of the stuff may not be worth bothering about.'

Zoe nodded. 'I'll have to sort them into categories first. Our own people can cover silver, china, and furniture, and Granville knows a lot about coins. There is some stuff we'll need outside experts to take a look at.'

'Like?'

'There are quite a few weapons, ancient and modern, some paintings and tapestries, and there's a library full of books that might be worth checking. There may be first editions mixed among all the others. There are even a couple of really old cars in the garage as well as some old farm machinery; they're bound to be worth something.'

'Well go ahead, sort them, and let our people have them. We'll go through the remains together when you've finished and see whom we should consult about them. By that stage we'll have an idea of what's worth selling and be able to judge whether it's worth sending an expert to check the library. I'll contact the family with a rough estimate and all the details and put them in the picture. They realized that it wouldn't be an overnight job, but I don't want to hang around too long.'

Zoe nodded. 'Okay, I'll get going right away. I'll keep you up to date. Anything else?' She got up and George shook his head.

On the way to the door, she stopped in her tracks when he said, 'Oh, yes! I nearly forgot. Alex Harding phoned when you were away. It appears that they were in port somewhere, picking up supplies, and he wanted to keep us informed. He phoned your office, but Don redirected the call to me. I've never spoken to him before. He asked where you were, what you were doing, sent his best wishes, etcetera.'

Zoe stared at the milky glass in the door and was glad she wasn't facing George. She turned and sounded quite calm. 'Oh! Any good news about the search?'

'He seemed quite optimistic. He told

me they'd found the exact spot where they believe the ship went down. Now they're checking the scatter pattern and taking crosscurrents into account that cut the area into sections. He had to explain what he was talking about. He mentioned the next step was charting the area and then searching it section by section.'

Zoe hoped her face didn't give her away. 'That sounds encouraging, doesn't it?'

'Mustn't get up too much hope, I suppose, but it didn't sound too bad. I told Don to put any other calls from him through to me, but you can take them yourself now if you like. You know him better than I do.'

She waved her hand. 'No, that's not necessary. I know that you'll keep me informed if you hear anything new.'

22

Zoe phoned Lucy and they arranged to meet that evening. Their local pub was busy but they were lucky and grabbed a corner table.

Once they had their drinks, Lucy deposited her capacious bag on the side and said, 'Come on then. Tell me exactly what happened.'

'I told you what happened on the phone.'

'You don't think I'm satisfied with that, do you? There weren't enough details.'

Zoe sighed and gave in. She told the finer points about the other ship, the grotty state of the cabin, how the two girls had supported each other, and how they'd eventually been rescued. By then their glasses were empty.

A couple of men at a nearby table ogled them, but for once Lucy didn't take any notice. She grabbed their empty glasses and hurried to the bar to get replacements. On her return she uttered, 'I just can't believe it. Here was I envying you all that sun and leisure, and all the time you were in the hands of some real villains.'

'On board Alex's ship it was fun, and afterwards when they rescued us and it was all over, it was okay too. The only black spot was the time in between on the other ship.'

'And what about the other woman? What was her name — Maria? When you mentioned her last time, you told me she had her fangs out because she thought you might be after Alex.'

'Yes but things improved, even before they took us hostage. I told her I wasn't interested in Alex and that seemed to help. Being in a situation like that also breaks down all kinds of barriers. You're in the same horrible place, facing the same problems.'

'They didn't try anything on, these men?'

'You mean physically? I've a feeling neither of us would still be around to tell the tale if things went wrong. Surprisingly, they kept their hands off us, apart from one day when one of them tried to grab Maria. Their leader sorted him out, and that was shortly before we were rescued.'

Lucy took a gulp. 'Hmm! Thank God nothing horrible happened. The whole thing is so unbelievable. It's odd though, isn't it? Why pick on you two? Didn't you tell me before you went out there for the second time that the crew thought someone who wanted to nab the treasure was following them? And why did they grab you?'

'They thought that if they had us as hostages, they could blackmail Alex into getting what they wanted without a fight, and without much effort. I was there by chance so they took me too.'

'I suppose so.' Lucy paused. 'And . . . did anything spark between you and him this time round? Did you fall for Mr. Superman?'

Willing herself not to give anything away, she met her glance straight on and said, 'You mean Alex?'

Lucy nodded.

'No. In fact, this time I even told him I didn't like his attitude and wasn't interested.'

'Wow! He looks luscious. Did you use exactly those words?'

'Not exactly, but he understood all right. I like him, but I kept my distance. Maria doesn't seem to mind that he flutters from butterfly to butterfly. She thinks she has him all figured out. She's welcome to him.'

'And you weren't attracted? It sounds like he's someone with real charisma if he has that kind of effect on women.'

'He's physically attractive and he does know how to manipulate women.' Zoe was picturing the anger in his gaunt face last time she saw him. She looked down and took another gulp of her lager. She had to change the subject fast or give herself away. 'What about you? What have you done since we last met? You had a date with that landscape gardener the day I left, didn't you? How did that work out?'

'Don't mention it, please. I have never spent a more boring evening in all my life.' Checking the perfect shine on her orange fingernails, she said, 'He seemed to think I was deadly interested in propagating a special variety of marigolds or some other useless flower. I don't know what I did to start him off, but once he got started I couldn't get a word in edgewise.'

Zoe laughed, relieved that they were talking about something else. 'Flowers are wonderful, and I think marigolds are often used for medical purposes. I must admit I didn't believe he was your type when you first mentioned him. Somehow I couldn't imagine you dead-heading the roses in a cottage in the country.'

'I can't either. I could imagine me dead-heading him though.'

'Poor man!'

'I have a date this weekend with a

Scotsman. I met him in the foyer of our company, and was bamboozled on the spot. He made me laugh in a matter of minutes. He had an appointment but was early, so he told me about his journey down from Edinburgh. I think he has a great sense of humour, and as he's only here until Sunday, he hoped I'd have pity on a lonely soul and spend one evening with him.'

'Not so good though, if he turns out to be Mr Right.'

'I've almost given up hoping to find Mr Right. You've infected my way of thinking. I'm planning to ask him what he wears under his kilt.'

Zoe laughed. 'Don't be shocked when he tells you. I think some Scottish men are very traditional, if you know what I mean. Did you tell him he had to wear a kilt when you go out?'

With a twinkle in her eye, Lucy said, 'He was wearing one already, that's what attracted me to him in the first place. I'm actually wondering if he'll shock me. How about me asking him if he knows someone he can bring with him? Then we could make up a foursome.'

Thinking quickly for a suitable excuse, Zoe told her, 'I've promised Mum I'd visit this weekend. I haven't been home for months. She knows I've been flitting back and forth to the Caribbean and she's impressed and wants some details.'

'Well, it was rather romantic until they kidnapped the two of you. Have you told her that you've invested some of your money in this scheme? Does she know you spent two days locked away as a hostage?'

'No, and don't you mention it next time you meet her either.'

'If she knew the truth, she'd flip her lid.'

'I don't want them to know. She'd be terribly shocked, and she'd start lecturing me about leaving London and looking for a job closer to home.'

'And that would be a bundle of fun, returning to the provinces and ending up a spinster of the parish. Stay here with me, love, where it's all happening.'

'I will, but this weekend I'm going home to relax and enjoy my family.'

23

Billy had a smile on his face three miles wide. 'You said it was here, but I admit, I was sceptical. Even after you told us why, and showed us the maps and information, I still couldn't believe that we'd find anything after more than three hundred and fifty years.'

Alex looked pretty satisfied. 'Then why did you risk your money?'

'You were certain. I had plenty of time on my hands, and nowhere to go. And . . . damn it, I like you.'

They could hear the others talking excitedly about the finds further down the deck. On the planking in front of them were the first costly items from the remains of the wreck. There were a couple of badges, a gold and emerald ring, and some small gold bars. They'd also found some oriental porcelain. How that had got on board an English man-of-war was a mystery, but perhaps the crew had boarded an enemy ship in the past and taken it as part of the booty. Perhaps the captain had served previously in oriental waters and they were his personal possessions. Alex picked up the ring to examine it more closely and the stones glistened brightly in the sunshine.

'Amazing that it still looks so good after all this time. There's more down there, a lot more. We'll break off for today and celebrate a little, but first thing tomorrow morning the sifting and clearing begins again in earnest. We'll have to widen the search area. Items could be strewn around if the storm raged for a long time. The ship could have broken apart slowly, bit by bit. I want to comb the whole area before anyone else gets wind of it. When they do, there is a real danger the scavengers will descend pretending to just be interested, but looking for a chance to make a claim.'

'Do you think the sailors on board survived?'

Alex shrugged. 'There was nothing about survivors in the records. If any managed to reach the shore alive after the storm, it was never reported.'

Billy viewed him. 'You're a stubborn mule, aren't you? You were determined to find it.'

Alex raised an eyebrow. 'It's one fault of which I've never been cured. My mother always complained about it.'

'Your stubbornness also seems to be causing you heartache. Forget your pride and think about what's really important.'

Alex viewed him carefully. 'I can guess what you're talking about. Sometimes it's better to concede defeat and move on. Eventually you forget, and you keep your pride and integrity intact.'

'What's that worth when you're miserable? A brief explanation about Maria would have cleared the air, and changed everything.'

'Why should I justify myself? I intended to talk to all of you and clear the situation, but she took off before I had a chance to do so. She doesn't trust me or accept me for what I am. I don't intend to beg her, or anyone else, for anything.'

'But she didn't know the truth. We all kept her in the dark about Maria because we didn't know her. She's also not the type of woman who'd pinch someone else's man. Cos that's what she thinks you are, Maria's boyfriend. She's not a mind-reader, Alex.'

'Would that have solved things? She wasn't just bothered about Maria; she was also bothered about references to other women in my past. Women she knows nothing about.'

He rubbed his chin. 'Boy, do you have a lot to learn about women! I bet you that every single woman has a problem living with the ghosts of predecessors. You admit yourself that you've been playing the field during the last couple of years. What kind of impression does that make on someone like her? She believed what we wanted her to believe, and she put two and two together when she heard about past girlfriends and made five out of it. She's someone who thinks carefully about what she's doing, and the effects. That makes her strong and also vulnerable.'

The frown on Alex's brow deepened. He rested his hands on his hips. 'Women don't act as you expect them to, do they? I know that Zoe is honest and candid, but she's too sensitive. I don't intend to justify my past just to please her.'

'Then all I can say is that you don't like her enough. Otherwise you'd move heaven and earth to straighten things out between the two of you.'

'You may be right, but then again you may be wrong.'

'Take my word for it, if you really love someone, you won't forget. Remember my wife? We were married twenty years, and if that train crash hadn't happened, we'd still be married today. Not a day passes without me thinking about her. If you don't have that kind of feeling for Zoe then it'd be better to forget her.

Better for you and better for her.'

Alex knew he was trying to ignore feelings he never expected to have, but he wasn't going to admit that to Billy. Given time, he'd forget her completely. 'Let's join the others, before the beer all disappears.'

Billy said no more. He followed him, and they joined in the celebration about the day's finds.

24

George popped his head round Zoe's door. 'Just had a phone call from Alex Harding. It looks like they've hit the jackpot.'

Just hearing someone mention his name gave her the collywobbles. She thought she had things under control and was beginning to forget him. It seems she wasn't. 'Really? That's great.'

'Quite a lot of stuff, apparently. They had to come into port somewhere to top up on supplies, and he used the chance to get in touch again. He said the main part of the area has been sifted through. They've now started examining the outer edges of the wreck area, in case things were spread around by currents or by the original storm.'

Zoe leaned back in her chair. 'That's super. They deserve their success. What have they found?'

'Gold chains, several rings, some brooches, badges and other jewellery, gold and silver bars, silver coins, doubloons, gold toothpicks, porcelain, as well as utensils like pottery, bottles, pipes, glasses, dishes, cannons and cannon balls. It sounds like a real haul of booty.'

'The captain must have seized some of that stuff from a foreign ship that was on its way home to Spain or Portugal. Alex explained that normally you wouldn't find much of value on a ship of her majesty's navy, so these things probably came from another ship. Officially, England wasn't at war with either Spain or Portugal, but the crown turned a blind eye as long as they brought back treasure. If no one can pinpoint the actual ship it came from, or the name of the captain, Alex will be able to claim the lot. It would be a lot more complicated if any other country was entitled to claim the stuff was theirs. They'd need to prove their ship was in the area at the time and under attack, but if both ships went down and there were no survivors, who can prove anything? Without logbooks it's almost impossible to prove positions or ownership in a case like this. If a government does have proof, and lays claim, the searchers sometimes end up with a pittance.'

'I haven't told William yet,' George said. 'He'll do a jig when I do. No one knows what this will bring from the money point of view, but at least everyone who invested in the expedition is likely to get their money back and a little extra.'

Zoe nodded. 'And everything else is going well?'

'So it seems. They'll be finished in a week or two and then Alex said he'd be in touch again. He asked where you were, and I explained you'd passed everything on to me, that's why his call ended up on my desk. He sent his best wishes. I told him how delighted everyone would be, but we wouldn't do anything about making it public until he thinks there's nothing more to find, and he can tell us exactly what they've found. You were right! You said from the very beginning that the search would succeed, and it did. The publicity, when everything is auctioned, will be tremendous.'

Zoe nodded and watched George leave. She stared into space and wished she could be with the crew as a silent observer. She'd missed the most exciting part of the search, but she still felt part of it all.

25

A couple of days later, George informed Zoe that Alex had been in touch again and a conference via Skype was arranged for the following afternoon. William had benignly decided she should be present after George had pointed out it was Zoe's idea in the first place, that she'd been involved from the very start, and she'd been on board twice and knew them all.

Zoe thought she was over Alex but clearly, from the feeling of half-anticipation, half-dread, she wasn't. She just hoped that some kind of coping mechanism would kick in. She took too much care in choosing what to wear, and arrived at the appointed time to stand next to George, looking at them all in the Caribbean via William's computer screen. They looked very tanned and happy.

Zoe's eyes were drawn to Alex

straight away, and her heart jolted. She tried in vain to throttle the emotions that erupted inside her, and was glad she only needed to be a silent observer. The crew, including Alex, ignored William and George straight away and shouted 'Hi Zoe!' Zoe waved back and tried to steady her thoughts. William redirected their attention by immediately plying them with questions. The mere sound of Alex's voice gave her butterflies in her stomach. She was too busy watching him to pay much attention to the conversation. Eventually she pulled herself together and concentrated.

'We've checked all of the area where I suspect there was something,' he said. 'We're all satisfied with what we've found so far. Since I last spoke to you, the number of items has increased. We now have several full crates of stuff. A day after we last spoke we found a silver candelabra, a couple of candlesticks and a lot more pottery and china. Presumably it all came from the officers' mess of the captured ship.'

William's eyes were shining. 'Splendid. So, in fact you've finished the actual search?'

'More or less. There can't be much more there now. I'll get in touch with the authorities to confirm the legalities, and when that's done, we'll get the stuff crated and airlifted to your company. Okay?'

'Yes, perfectly. My staff will examine each item and begin to estimate and prepare descriptions for a catalogue. I hope there'll be enough to hold an exclusive auction with your finds. George is sure the media interest will be terrific. We'll decide about that after we see how much, and what.'

Alex nodded and smiled. Zoe had a lump in her throat. She'd really believed she was over him, but she wasn't. Her love was only lying dormant beneath the surface.

He said, 'We don't think it's sensible to send valuable items through the usual channels. We've talked about it, and decided that we'll need some kind of special security delivery.'

'Agreed, and don't forget you'll need to clear everything with customs. There's no point in just turning up with an antique candelabra under your arm.'

'That's one of the things I intend to sort out in the next couple of days.'

'Can we help from this end? George or Zoe will be glad to help if they can.'

He shook his head. 'Not at the moment.'

Zoe felt she needed to say something. She leaned over William's shoulder. 'Congratulations! It's really great news.'

Billy, standing at Alex's shoulder, chuckled. 'Yes, it is. We've thoroughly enjoyed the last couple of weeks. Not a single day passed without us finding something. Alex was spot-on with his guess.'

Standing with his hands stuck in his pockets, Alex remained silent but Hank butted in. 'If we hadn't had that problem with you and Maria, it would have been a perfect search. We would have also kept our cook. You wouldn't believe the insults I've had to put up with since you left, Zoe.'

She laughed. 'Well you all look very well. Your cooking skills can't be that bad.'

Maria hurried to add, 'How are you, Zoe? Have you got over our forced custody?'

'I'm fine, thanks. And you?'

'Couldn't be better. The police haven't caught them yet, but they know the name of the leader of the gang. He's disappeared though, so it'll be a matter of luck if any of them are ever brought to justice.'

'Somehow I thought it would be difficult to find them. They were too well organized.'

William stirred in his seat; Zoe reckoned he was getting bored because he wasn't getting the prominence he expected. 'I hope to see you all again. Will you be coming to London?'

Gary nodded. 'For the auction. Most of us have never been to the UK so it's a perfect chance.'

Alex added, 'Once I've sorted out the initial problems, I'll be in touch again.'

William replied, 'Yes, do that. George will handle everything and he'll keep me informed. Well done, and good to speak to you all.'

Alex nodded and they all shouted 'Bye!' with an extra 'Bye, Zoe!' for her benefit.

William closed the connection. Zoe mused that no one had actually asked them where they were. Perhaps they didn't want to broadcast it until they'd cleared up all the details and legalities.

Usually, Zoe wanted to be involved in any job she'd been in on from the beginning. This time she was glad to leave George and William to it. She was happier to be alone with her thoughts. Seeing Alex had been wonderful and also punishing. He looked so good, and very fit. He was taller than the other men and he had a kind of inherent strength in his attitude that was mirrored in the expression on his ruggedly handsome face. The way he stood showed he was the focal point of the group. He didn't need to pretend he was in charge. The sunlight glinted on his hair, and his washed-out jeans and T-shirt merely heightened his attraction in her eyes. He looked so good and so tough. He was a rock in a stormy sea. She knew she viewed him with biased eyes, but she loved him more than she thought possible.

Could she hide her feelings when they met again? Could she remain logical and down-to-earth when it was clear that she lost control of her thoughts every time she saw him? At least William and George had been with her staring at the computer screen this morning. She hoped the group of them in the Caribbean were concentrated on listening to them, and didn't notice her bemused expression. What if Alex decided to bring across the most valuable items himself?

26

As it turned out, Zoe wasn't in the office when an international security firm delivered the most costly items. She was on holiday with Lucy. They'd chewed over the idea of touring France and moving from place to place according to the weather and their inclinations. It wasn't the best time to visit because soon the whole of France would be on holiday. The week before they were due to leave, they were poring over brochures and other information in Lucy's flat.

Zoe commented, 'We'll have to decide soon. The ferries are booked out at this time of year. Everyone is going on holiday.'

Pretending not to sound eager, Lucy said, 'Or shall we go somewhere else?'

'Like?'

Fiddling with a rubber band, she

replied, 'I don't know. We could stay here. Or Wales, perhaps? The Lake District? Cornwall? Scotland?'

Zoe felt amused. Lucy was still interested in her Scottish boyfriend. Clearly, she liked him more than she cared to admit. He'd attracted her ever since his first business trip to London. Since then, they phoned each other regularly, and Lucy had visited him in Edinburgh one weekend. She hadn't gone into much detail when she returned, but she did declare that the city was fab and she'd had a great time. Zoe didn't push for more information, but she wondered if Lucy was star-struck about someone at last.

'Has this anything to do with Andrew, by any chance?'

Lucy looked flustered. 'No, of course not. We don't have to go to Scotland; it was only a suggestion.'

Zoe got up from her chair and hugged her friend. 'Don't be silly. Why not admit that you'd like to see him again? If you like him that much, he must be special. Up until now, you've tarred and feathered nearly every boyfriend of yours that I've ever met. Andrew sounds nice, and if you're keen on him, a holiday in Scotland is fine by me. If we go together, it doesn't look like you're going because of him. Tell him we're coming and see how he reacts. Once we get there, and you want to be with Andrew, I'll be happy to go off on my own and visit the usual tourist attractions. What does he do, by the way?'

Slightly flushed and with bright eyes, she said, 'He's a lawyer.'

'Wow! That's quite a change from your usual flamboyant choices.'

'He's fun. Just because he's a lawyer doesn't mean he's the next thing to an undertaker!'

Zoe laughed. 'I'm sure he's great. He must be if you like him.'

'He is.'

'Then that's settled.' She bundled the papers on the coffee table into a pile and threw them in the bin. 'When I was in Scotland for the firm recently, I thought it was beautiful. I was in a remote place in the Highlands. It's not all Disneyland of course, but most of Scotland does have some fabulous scenery.'

'Andrew's parents come from one of the islands on the west coast.'

'They're supposed to be breath-taking. If you want to spend all your time with your irresistible Andrew, I'll disappear somewhere for a couple of days.'

'And you wouldn't mind?'

'Of course not.' Zoe didn't want to add that at the moment the idea of playing gooseberry to two people in love definitely wasn't very appealing. 'I'm looking forward to meeting him. Are you going to dress yourself in Scottish tartan and take a course in Scottish country dancing before we go, or wait until after we get there?'

★   ★   ★

Andrew was nice; Zoe liked him straight away. He was good to look at, with a square, scraggy face and broad shoulders. His blue eyes twinkled and he had a likeable, endearing sense of humour. She had to admit there was something special about a man who wore a kilt, and he wore his with pride. Zoe wondered if he wore it when he attended court. She never saw him in anything else. Lucy clearly delighted in his company, and the way he looked at her and made gentle references to 'my little Sassenach' made Zoe decide they were on the way to falling in love.

After she'd met him, Zoe announced, 'I'd love to tour the west coast for a couple of days. I know you wanted to see more of Edinburgh, Lucy; would you mind if I leave you here and take off on my own?'

Andrew hurried to hide his delighted expression and then looked at Lucy. Cradling her glass, she replied, 'No, not if you really want to go. I'd like to see the west coast too, but there's still so much I'd like to see in Edinburgh. I'd rather stay here if you don't mind.'

Andrew added, 'I'll take some time off from work and it'll be a pleasure to show you around.'

Lucy coloured and nodded. 'That would be nice.'

Zoe had seldom seen Lucy look so contented, and Andrew seemed just as infatuated. Zoe finished her drink and pleaded tiredness, wanting to leave them on their own. She was happy for Lucy. It made her wistful about losing Alex, although she knew it wasn't a real loss because Alex had never been hers.

27

When Zoe returned to London, routine kicked in again. The summer weather was still good and London was full of tourists. The pressure of work wasn't so much of a problem because most people chose to buy or sell in the cooler months of the year. The preparation for one future auction in particular was in full swing — the finds from Alex's treasure hunt.

George put Zoe in the picture. 'The costly stuff has already been estimated and photographed. Descriptions are in the pipeline and we're beginning to put a catalogue together.'

Zoe was surprised. 'A special catalogue? So it's not going to be part of another auction then?'

'No. I persuaded William to keep it exclusive. It will bring us a lot more publicity. As soon as the catalogue is ready, we'll start a media campaign. Hopefully the press will jump on it like leeches. There isn't much sensational going on, or the usual crop of political disasters at the moment, so they'll probably be glad of something to fill their pages.'

'When do you think that we'll be ready? When are you planning the actual auction?'

'At the beginning of autumn.'

'Has it all arrived?'

'The pricey stuff came under special security weeks ago. I must say your friend Harding is very thorough. It was all listed piece by piece with photos, numbers and suggested descriptions. The other items — interesting but less costly stuff — have begun to arrive in the last couple of days. Some of it is quite sensational. I wouldn't be surprised if some museums bid for it.'

'He's not a friend, George, just one of the crew. He's cleared the legal hick-hack then?'

'Yes, he sorted out the British side of

it before he even began to look. Any claim by another foreign power needs proof. The items in question could have come from any ship sailing those waters. Even if there is a strong possibility it did come from a Spanish or Portuguese ship, they'd have to prove ownership in an international court, and that would be extremely difficult considering that both ships must have gone down in the same storm, perhaps in even completely different positions. Apparently, so far, there has been no other official claim. The fact that the ship was British is a proven fact, and all this stuff came from the wreck of this British ship. That can be proved. It'd be mere conjecture to declare that what they've found came from another source. The cannons provide the name of the ship and the name of its captain. The voyage is a registered fact. Anyone can own, buy or be given things that seem a bit exotic. They could have all been on board before the ship left England.'

'I'm glad it looks fairly cut and dried. It must be hell when a crew ends up having to fight their claims in court. Just imagine some government waltzing in and snapping it all away from under your nose after you've done all the research and put in all the elbow grease.'

George nodded. 'There's an international rewards system, but that's not the same as being entitled to the lot.'

She asked casually, 'Have you spoken to anyone from the crew since I was with you that time?'

'I've spoken to Harding several times via video conferencing. Once, when I needed to clear something fast, he flew over once for a quick visit to get a preview of the layout for the catalogue.'

Zoe's breath caught in her throat.

'That was when you were on holiday, of course. He asked where you were and I took him out to lunch. I liked him. We agreed that it would be a good idea to get media interest in advance to encourage buyers for the auction. I arranged a couple of press interviews during the time he was here, and it went down very well.'

'I haven't paid much attention to newspapers because of my holidays. Pity! I would have liked to read about their reaction.'

'I've still got some copies in the office. One of the daily ones gave it a good spread. I think he didn't fit the press's general idea of an adventurer searching for lost treasure. He emphasised the investigation side of it all — how thorough you need to be, and how you need expert advice as well. He also added that a well-balanced crew and good organization are the key to success. Clearly the press decided he wasn't an oddball, and knew what he was doing.'

She was deceptively calm. 'Did he mention what had happened to Maria and me?'

'No. We agreed beforehand that he wouldn't. You already told me you didn't want the publicity and he said he wanted to stop the press hounding the other woman too. The crew guessed she might already be spotlighted because she's female, but she'll remain officially just one of the crew. If the gutter press wittered something sensational was in the offing, a thwarted kidnapping is just what they'd want. We want a serious presentation and we'll stick to the facts.'

Zoe nodded. 'That's right. The fact that we supported the search financially isn't important anymore, but how we handle the auction will secure the company's future for a while. I haven't seen William since I got back. Where is he?'

'Today? He's sacrificing himself to play golf with a prospective client somewhere in Sussex. He's skiving again.'

★ ★ ★

When the day of the auction dawned, Zoe was more nervous than she'd ever been before. Not because of the auction, but because she'd be seeing Alex again and she wasn't sure if she could cope. How would she react and feel when they came face to face?

The doors opened officially at ten o'clock. Several members of staff were on duty and Zoe was designated to help George wherever he needed her. The trickle turned into a steady flow. They were all surprised by the number of reporters who turned up with their notebooks and accompanying camera-men.

Tipping her chin in the direction of the reporters, she said, 'Where's William? He generally likes to be at the centre of any free publicity.'

George shrugged his shoulders. 'Still drinking coffee, I expect. I don't expect to see him until someone wants an official comment from us. He's waiting to find out if the auction is just a success, or a resounding success. When that happens I bet that he'll turn up and deliver a speech proclaiming how he was always closely involved and firmly believed it would end splendidly.' He looked at his watch. 'I'd better go out front and grab Alex and the others when they arrive. I told Granville to reserve them some seats — first row and dead centre.'

Zoe's pulse increased. George disappeared and she moved to the side. Sounds buzzed, telephones tinkled with various calling tunes, and the place was soon full to capacity. It was hot and stuffy. Zoe helped someone to open doors and windows. She looked at her watch nervously, bracing herself to see Alex and the crew. She could tell they'd arrived long before she spotted them, when the lights began to blaze and murmuring voices reached a new excited peak. When Zoe finally saw them, she thought they looked wonderfully tanned and relaxed. She searched frantically between the moving crowds and cameras held above everyone's heads to see Alex. He was above average height and once the initial photos were done, Zoe saw him moving towards the front to their places in the front row.

She took a deep breath and knew that her face was bright pink. She was glad she had time to hide her agitation and adjust before she spoke to them. Even though he wasn't hers, she felt a warm glow in the knowledge he was here, in the same room. She reminded herself the auction had priority over other things today, and she opened her catalogue as George mounted the auction block and began to speak.

Sometimes in the past, she'd acted as clerk at George's auctions, but she was glad that Granville was handling the paperwork this morning. He sat at a table facing the audience, directly next to the block where George began his explanation.

'Good morning, ladies and gentlemen. We'd like to welcome you to today's auction. I think most of you have already read all about the origins of the items on offer this morning. Mr. Alex Harding and the rest of his crew found them on his latest expedition in the Caribbean. I'm sure if you've gone through the catalogue and seen the items, you'll agree that they are exceptional, and very interesting finds. I think it's not necessary for me to emphasise that nobody should bid unless they want to make a genuine offer. We don't want to waste anyone's time.' He paused and gestured briefly. 'I would particularly like to welcome Mr. Harding and the members of his crew, who made the journey especially to be here today.' A hand, Alex's, acknowledged briefly the round of applause. 'Good. I'd like to inform you that we have absentee bidders for several items. I will notify you when someone has made a bid in this manner whenever applicable. Unless anyone has a question they'd like to clear before we start, we'll get down to business — auctioning the treasure and various artefacts from the wreck of the *Admiral Bowden*. Can I have the first minimum opening bid for item number one, please? It's a very fine example of a dress sword, in excellent condition, with a silver hilt and guard. This was in all probability the property of one of the officers on board.'

Someone lifted his bidding card and the auction began in earnest. Now and then Zoe stood on tiptoe trying to glimpse the group. Apart from the backs of their heads, there wasn't much to see. They were obviously following the auction with interest. George announced a break after two hours. Coffee and biscuits were on offer in the adjoining room.

Zoe was taken aback when someone unexpectedly grabbed her and lifted her off the floor with work-roughened hands. She looked into Billy's face and laughter shone in their eyes as they viewed each other.

'Put me down, you old sea-dog.'

He chuckled. 'How's my favourite girl?'

'Fine, and you?'

'Hunky-dory. Especially when I sit

there counting up what that stuff is worth. Even after commission and repaying the investments, there's still going to be a decent amount to be shared out.'

Zoe nodded. 'And the best is still to come. Our chief auctioneer has naturally saved the most expensive items till the end.'

He looked around. 'So this is where you work?'

'Yes. What do you think?'

'You shouldn't ask a sailor something like that. I'd go crazy if I had to spend my time in a place like this.'

'Ah! But there wouldn't be any point in you finding treasure if no one is there to buy it afterwards, would there? This is a traditional auction house. It's been in the same family for a couple of generations.'

'That's what it looks like too. It could do with a lick of paint.'

She chuckled and looked up at his craggy face. 'Oh, I have missed you and the sun and being in the tropics at the end of a long summer day. I'll never forget the colours of the soft twilight.' She paused. 'How are the others? I hear Alex visited the office recently, when I was on holiday.'

'Yes, he told me you were on holiday. We're fine. You'll be able to have a chat with everyone when this is all over. We're being bombarded with questions by complete strangers, and I think the auctioneer has organized a question-and-answer time for later.'

'Yes, George — he's my boss — told me about that. It's all publicity, Billy. Our firm needs all that it can get. Competition is fierce these days.'

He studied her carefully. 'You've lost a little weight, haven't you?'

'I did a lot of walking when I was on holiday. I went to Scotland. It was beautiful.'

'You should have come out to see us instead.'

'You were up to your eyeballs in sorting everything out. Nothing is more annoying than having to look after a visitor when you have too much to do yourself.'

He ruffled her hair. 'You wouldn't be a visitor. You're one of us.'

Zoe looked into his kind face. 'Thanks, Billy. You're a gem.'

He shuffled. 'I'd better get Maria a cup of coffee. That's how I managed to escape the attention of a woman dripping in jewellery and with a face like a dried lemon.'

'The coffee is next door.' She pointed the way. 'I'll see you after the auction.'

He tipped his forehead with his finger and left her to make his way through the throng into the next room.

When the auction restarted, gold jewellery, precious stones, various silver items including a fantastic silver candelabra, and coins were up for sale. Zoe's mouth fell open a couple of times at the sums people paid. She knew that a scattering of museums were interested and had made pre-bids. Gradually George worked his way down the list until the final moment when he knocked down the last item with a determined thump. Zoe knew already that the end sum would be tremendous. Alex, the crew, investors, and auction house could be delighted with the payoff. She thought briefly about her own investment.

Most people stayed seated when George announced that Alex and the crew were being ushered onto the podium to answer questions. The press then proceeded to ask for more details about how, when, why and where. It was the first time Zoe had the chance to study Alex's face.

The corners of his mouth were pulled into a slender smile. She saw him checking the room and when he spotted her, he smiled more easily and gave her a special nod. His white teeth flashed briefly; they were dazzling against the olive tone of his skin. She looked at him, drinking in the sight of him, before she finally smiled back. He returned his attention to answering the questions that were thrown in his direction by the surrounding press. His voice sent a ripple of awareness through her and she was amazed that it had such an effect. The questions bounced back and fore among the crew. The cameras flashed and the press was particularly interested in questioning Maria.

Someone asked, 'Were you apprehensive about being the only female on board?'

'No, of course not. I knew all the men beforehand, and I've worked with men all my life. My father is a deep-sea diver, and I could swim before I could walk. The men just accepted me as one of the crew and I didn't expect any extra attention just because I'm a woman. I'm good at my job and they knew it. Now that the search has been brought to a successful conclusion I'll be able to fulfil a lifetime wish. My fiancé and I are planning to open a diving school in Hawaii.' She flashed a large emerald engagement ring at the cameras. 'That's something else this search has brought me — a fiancé.'

The flashlights lit up the room as the press pounced on a particularly human aspect of the expedition. The story would go down well.

28

Zoe leaned back against the wall and felt almost faint. Her throat was raw with unuttered protest, and she felt how grief tore at her. In dismay she admitted she should have thought of the possibility, but she hadn't. Alex wasn't someone who'd be easily trapped, but Maria had managed it. Facing them now on the podium just made her intensely miserable. She turned away quickly, not wanting to see or hear any more. A kind of panic began to grow within her. She had to escape.

She half-stumbled her way down the empty corridor to the lift and up to her room. She was glad she met no one on the way. Slumping into her office chair, she swallowed the despair and willed herself not to cry. Somehow she must pull herself together and cope. One thing was certain: she couldn't face

Maria and Alex today; first she had to reconcile herself to the news first. She'd send them written congratulations and that would have to do for the moment. She couldn't meet Billy and the other men without Alex and Maria, so that meant she had to avoid them all. It was a pity because it was unlikely that she'd meet any of them again once they left.

She drank some water from the dispenser in the corridor and fought hard against emerging tears. She refused to give in. She needed an escape route and reached for her appointment book. A wave of relief swept over her when she saw she had a meeting with an antique dealer in Dover tomorrow morning. Grabbing a pen and a notebook, she wrote,

Dear George,

I've just remembered I have a meeting with someone tomorrow at 8.30 a.m. I'm going to travel down this evening and check into a local hotel. I need to be punctual tomorrow morning because this chap is

known to be pedantic. I need to pack a bag before I leave, so will you please tell the crew and Alex that I'm awfully sorry and very disappointed that I won't be able to meet them after all? Please also pass on my congratulations to the engaged couple. Great news! The auction was a wonderful success and we'll have a good chat about it when I get back. I'll keep you informed.
Thanks,
Zoe.

She ripped it out, stuck it in an envelope, and grabbed her bag and her jacket on the run. Hurrying downstairs, she skirted the auction room where the interview was still in progress. Eric the janitor was standing near the entrance. 'Eric, will you give this note to George as soon as you see him, please? It's very important that he gets it today before he leaves.'

Eric took the envelope. 'Of course. It looks like it won't be long before the auction breaks up now. Some people have already left.'

Nodding, she hoped her voice didn't sound too stilted or unnatural. 'Have they? You won't forget, will you?'

'No, of course not. You have my word.'

Rushing past him out into the street, Zoe was glad to be alone; and as soon as she reached a nearby square with a sprinkling of greenery, she sank down on a bench and gave in to her misery. She loved Alex desperately and had never wanted anyone in this way before. She'd been strong enough to break away in the Caribbean, and she'd be strong enough to get on with her life again in the UK too. But she felt wretched. The tears fell as she scrabbled around in her bag for a handkerchief. She was glad the square was empty and the houses silent and unpopulated. Forcing herself to take several deep breaths, she wiped her tears and tried to think sensibly again.

She'd stick to her plan. Her appointment tomorrow was genuine, even if she'd arranged to meet the prospective client later than she'd stated. She couldn't stay in London. The crew might ask where she lived, then phone and try to persuade her to join them. She got up and made her way home. Packing an overnight holdall, she kept her eye on the clock. The misery was still foremost in her emotions, but having something to do helped to occupy her brain a little. She felt relief when she was finally in her car and on the south circular road. It started to rain, and as the wipers thrashed their way back and forth across the windscreen, Zoe let her thoughts tumble. Life would go on. She didn't know how yet, but she'd find a way. A glance at her watch reminded her that when she got to Dover she had to phone Lucy. They usually met on a Monday.

After she'd checked into the small hotel, she took an umbrella from the boot and wandered the streets. Anything was better than just lying on her bed in the hotel. She wasn't hungry and when she got back to the hotel, she went to the bar for a coffee. There were no other guests, and as soon as her cup was empty she went to her room to spend a sleepless night.

29

The auction room emptied. The reporters were on their way back to present their editors with a story for tomorrow's issue. Alex and the others were gathered in a loose group around George.

He looked baffled. 'I don't know where she is. She was here earlier on. She was here for the whole auction. I'm sure she also mentioned that she planned to meet you all afterwards. I'll go and find out if anyone else has seen her or spoken to her.' He hurried off.

Alex turned to Billy. 'You spoke to her and she didn't say anything about having something else on her schedule, did she?'

Billy shook his head. 'No, she said she'd see us all later. She seemed glad to see me and everything seemed okay.'

He glared. 'Then what the hell is she

playing at? We're all expecting her to come out with us this evening.'

'She's not playing round. You know her better than that. Something changed her plans.' Billy could tell Alex was angry and more concerned than he cared to admit. 'There must be a logical explanation.'

The skin was drawn taunt over his cheekbones and his eyes were icy. 'What about the option that she just wants to avoid me? She's been deliberately avoiding me ever since the day she persuaded the police to take her back to the mainland.'

Billy pulled him aside. The others were still excitedly discussing the day's happenings, so they didn't notice. Scratching his head, Billy said, 'She was looking forward to seeing everyone, and that included you. You haven't had a chance to meet until today, have you? She was friendly to you on that video conference. It was unlucky that you came when she was on holiday but you should have checked that first. She didn't arrange not to be here, I don't believe that.'

Alex's voice was sharp. 'Why not? Perhaps she can't stand the sight of me anymore.'

There was challenge in Billy's voice. 'She's not the sort of woman to deliberately avoid anyone unless she has a good reason. If you feel anything for her, you need to sort it out soon. Something is wrong here. She isn't the kind to run away from anyone. If you can live with not seeing her again, and it won't bother you if you don't see her for the rest of your life, then just forget her and get on with your life. Otherwise you have to find her and find out what's bothering her. It's up to you.'

Alex glowered and his face had an unfamiliar angry look. Whatever he was about to say was lost when he saw George hurrying back.

Waving an envelope in their faces, he said, 'She left a message. She remembered about an important meeting with a client, very early tomorrow morning.

She'd decided to drive there this evening, to be certain she'll be on time for the appointment. The chap seems to be a bit of a stickler. Anyway . . . she asked me to tell you she's very disappointed she can't meet you as arranged and she also asked me to pass on her congratulations on the engagement.' He smiled. 'I presume she'll be in touch later.'

'Later? I'm not sure if there'll be a later.' Alex turned on his heel and strode off into the corridor.

Billy tried to soothe the situation. 'Alex's not being rude. I think he's just disappointed. I'd better go after him and try to calm things again.'

Looking surprised, George nodded. As an afterthought, Billy hesitated and asked, 'Did Zoe talk about Alex much?'

'You mean personally?' He pondered. 'I'm not sure, but come to think about it, she was always very brief whenever his name cropped up. Is something wrong? Have they quarrelled?'

Billy brushed his words aside. 'No,

nothing to worry about. I was just curious, that's all.'

'When are you planning to return to the States?'

'Alex wants to show us around for a couple of days. Not that we need much persuasion. London is quite a city.'

'Then I'd like to take you all out for a meal before you leave. Lunch or dinner, just as you like. Where are you staying? I'll phone Alex and arrange something with him.'

Billy had to think. 'The hotel is called West End. A nice little place. Not too big, and it has a nice cosy atmosphere. Alex knew we wouldn't feel happy in one of those glass and steel towers.'

'Yes, I know it. It's more traditional. Tell Alex I'll phone him tomorrow. I'm looking forward to reading about the auction. You are too, I expect.'

Billy laughed. 'Yes, and we're all look-ing forward to finding out how much money we made too. Bye, George.' He lifted his hand and went to look for Alex and the others.

30

Zoe had a brief, fruitful meeting with the customer. He seemed interested in putting some furniture into one of their next auctions, and Zoe left him with all the details and the reassurance that he had plenty of time to consider before he made a definite decision. She'd already checked out of the hotel, so she was free to leave straight after the meeting ended.

She'd been glad to concentrate on work for a while. It kept her thoughts on a sensible course. Looking at her white face in the rear mirror of her car, she could tell that even if she'd managed to trick her mind for a while, her body wasn't so easily swindled. She drew into the next petrol station and bought a cup of coffee. It was tasteless but at least it was hot.

She phoned George.

'Hey! How did it go?'

'Fine; he's thinking about it. I didn't push him. I think if I tried to pressure him, he would have pulled out. He has some beautiful Georgian stuff. It would look good in one of our auctions. How are things?'

He chuckled. 'The phone hasn't stopped ringing this morning, ever since the articles about the treasure hunt hit the street. People we once had as customers but lost have suddenly remembered us again.'

'There are articles in the paper? Already?'

'Most of the press were there. There were even a couple from specialist and lifestyle magazines, but the majority were normal newspaper reporters. Haven't you seen any papers this morning?'

'No, I didn't think about it.'

'Well take a look. Oh, your friends from the crew seemed very disappointed that you didn't join them after all. I explained of course. I aim to take them out for a meal before they leave. Perhaps you can join us?'

Zoe swallowed a lump in her throat. 'When are they leaving?'

'In a couple of days, Friday I think. I arranged to meet them Thursday lunchtime. They were planning to go to Hampton Court today. Billy was flabbergasted when he heard that Henry VIII had six wives. He wants to see the places where it all happened.'

She tried to sound cheerful. 'That'll keep them busy.'

'Take the day off, Zoe. By the time you get back it will be past lunchtime anyway. We can all afford to relax now that auction is over. They'll go home with a tidy sum. All of them.'

'That's a good idea. Thanks, George, I will. See you.'

'Yes; bye, Zoe.'

She was glad he hadn't insisted on her joining them for the meal. It would have been hard to find another excuse. She went back to the newspaper stand in the petrol station and picked out some newspapers at random. Back in the shelter and quiet of her car she ruffled through the pages, looking for relevant articles. She soon found some, with photos of the group and some showing a selection of auctioned items.

Her thoughts drifted back to the day she'd met Alex. She ought to phone Tony and ask him if he'd seen the newspapers. Tony had brought her and Alex together. She reminisced about how Alex had held her and kissed her, and how they'd enjoyed each other's company. She clung to all the other memories, although she knew it was futile and counterproductive. She had to forget him. Staring unseeingly through the windscreen, she knew she had to accept the inevitable; but at the moment, she wondered how she could face life knowing Alex and Maria were engaged and soon to be married. She told herself that someday in the future it wouldn't hurt anymore. She didn't want to see him again, and that meant she had to find a way to block any plan George might make to include her in the meal.

She drove home and unpacked, then did a few mundane household chores to occupy her mind; it helped to fill in the time. Checking the clock, she waited until she knew Lucy would be home from work. Then she phoned her and said she was coming around. She'd kept Lucy in the dark about the most important happening in her life and it was time to change that. Lucy would rally round, even though she could only listen and sympathise. At the moment, that was what she needed — someone to talk to and who understood her.

Beaming at her, Lucy opened the door. 'Hello, love.' Glancing at her friend's face, her smile faded and she said, 'What's up? You look like you've seen a ghost. Bad news? Something happen at home?'

Zoe shook her head. 'No, but I need to talk to you.' She dumped her bag on the side and sat down on the couch.

'Come on then, out with it. What's bothering you?'

Zoe told her, hesitatingly at first, how

she'd been attracted to Alex from the beginning; how she'd tried to ignore her feelings for him; how his kisses just made her want more, even though he was hooked on Maria. She even told Lucy she'd contemplated encouraging him but decided against it, knowing it would only be a short-lived affair. Finally, she told her how she'd run away via the police launch to get away from him, and thought she'd be able to cope with seeing him some time in the future. She had until he'd turned up yesterday, engaged to Maria.

Lucy just sat and listened. She didn't comment until Zoe was finally silent. 'I always had a feeling you were attracted to him, from your very first meeting. Later you avoided talking about him and didn't mention his name much. I must admit I thought that was strange and wondered why, because you also admitted that he was very attractive and interesting. I never pushed you for more information. We've always been good friends and I didn't want to interfere. I reasoned that if you thought there was anything special about Alex Harding, you'd tell me sooner or later. Perhaps I could have helped. Talking about problems with someone else always helps.' She sat down next to Zoe and hugged her. 'I'm so sorry. I wish I could put things right.'

With tears threatening to fall, Zoe gulped. 'I know. I should have told you earlier. It's not that I don't trust you. I didn't know how to cope and felt too confused to talk about it.'

Lucy patted her hand. 'Well you have now. Perhaps you'll get over him faster than you think, and feel a lot better about it.'

'I don't think so, even though it wasn't even a proper romance. Just a few kisses and an overwhelming feeling I had about him. He was the one I always hoped I would find one day. I couldn't tell anyone I was potty about someone who didn't return my feelings.'

'You could have told me. I would

have understood. It's awful to think you've felt miserable for weeks and weeks. Even before we went on holiday to Scotland?' Zoe nodded. 'That must have been dire, especially when things were working out between me and Andrew.'

Zoe sniffed and tried to feel happy for her friend. 'Are they working out? I'm so glad. Don't feel bad. I think it's great that you've found someone you like so much. You've always had such a lot of oddball boyfriends in the past. I like Andrew very much. I was surprised that you liked him in the beginning, because in comparison to you he's very down-to-earth, but he has a great sense of humour. I can tell how much you like each other.' Zoe brushed away any escaping tears with the back of her hand.

Lucy faltered, 'I was thinking of looking for a job up there to be near him but I'll put that off for a while. I couldn't leave you here now, not when you're feeling so miserable.'

With a voice that was still shaky, Zoe said, 'Don't be silly. Of course you must go, if that's what you want to do. You'll never know if you like each other enough by spending weekends together. Especially you. You've chopped and changed boyfriends too often. You need to be absolutely sure. I'll keep busy with evening classes, keep-fit, home decorating, and I'll visit you or you'll visit me. We won't lose contact.' She blew her nose and straightened her shoulders. 'Have you started looking yet?'

'No, but Andrew keeps sending me adverts that he thinks might suit, from the local newspaper.'

'Well, if there's a job you like the look of, why don't you apply? Don't risk losing Andrew. You like him too much already.'

'We'll see. What about a nice comforting chocolate drink?'

Zoe nodded, although she didn't want anything.

'And what are you planning to do?'

Lucy started to bustle around her tiny kitchen unit, gathering what she needed.

'Once I find a way to avoid meeting them, I'll be able to think straight again. George is inviting them out for a meal before they leave, and he might suggest I join them. Normally, I'd enjoy it.'

'But not anymore?'

Zoe's voice was full of anguish and the hurt was back in her eyes. 'What do you think? Can you imagine how I'd feel seeing Alex and Maria together? In a couple of months, when I've got used to the idea, I could manage it. But not now.' As an afterthought, she added, 'I don't suppose I'll see any of them again after they leave.'

Lucy handed her a mug. 'Just as you like it, with one spoon of sugar.' She was silent for a moment. 'Then for a start you should skip work until they've left. When are they going?'

'I think George mentioned Friday when he was telling me about the invite.'

'Then you'll have to find a way to skive off until they're gone. Can you use a genuine excuse? Something for a day or two? How about a meeting with an out-of-town client, something along those lines?'

Glumly she answered, 'I already used that as an excuse to escape last night. George will notice something is fishy if I try that again. If he checked my appointment book, he'd find I don't have a single thing scheduled for the rest of this week.' She put her mug on the coffee table and grabbed another paper hanky from the box. Tears trickled down her cheeks again and she rubbed at them determinedly. 'Hell! Why did I have to fall for a man who belongs to someone else?'

'Why is the world round, the grass green, or your boss a square stick-in-the-mud?'

'George isn't so bad. He's a decent boss and I like him. That's why I don't like cheating him.'

Lucy lifted her shoulders. 'There

isn't an easy way out. You only need a small fib. You've never cheated before and probably never will again. Tell you what — I'll phone him tomorrow morning and tell him you've suddenly been taken ill with flu and you've gone home to your mum and dad and hope to be back at work on Monday unless it develops into something more serious. I can't remember you being off sick since you came to London.'

'What about a doctor's note?'

'Oh, we'll bother about details like that later. You should disappear fast and not be available over the phone either. George may try to persuade you to at least meet the crew for the meal if he can reach you.'

'Oh, he wouldn't, would he?'

Lucy gave her another hug. 'He might even give one of the crew your address. You need to be out of reach and it'll do you good to get away for a couple of days. Your parents will be delighted to have you for a day or two.'

Zoe began to feel the first threads of

hope since yesterday afternoon. Lucy's idea wasn't bad. At the moment she didn't even care much if she lost her job. Life went on. Once the fuss had settled, she could even start to find a new job. She'd miss the people she worked with, but a new job would be a challenge and keep her busy. She met Lucy's glance and nodded. 'Okay.'

'Good. First, we'll go round to your flat and pack a holdall for a couple of days. Then we'll go down the pub for a meal, and finally come back here and crack open a bottle of wine. I don't think you should go whizzing down the motorway right away. The rain is bucketing down at present and it's appalling driving conditions. You'd have water outside and inside your car. You'll also give your parents a hell of a shock if you turn up in the middle of the night. You can sleep here. We'll both have headaches tomorrow morning, but never mind! I'll phone George when I get to work. By then you'll be well on your way.'

Zoe viewed her friend and she was glad she'd told her. Facing reality with Lucy was definitely better than facing it alone.

31

Zoe spent the night on the couch and had a crick in her neck when she woke up. She waved Lucy a sleepy goodbye and then got ready. Half an hour and one cup of coffee later, she was on her way. The early morning traffic was heavy, but once she reached the outer edges of the ring road it thinned a bit and she joined the M4. When she stopped for a break after a while, she phoned her mother.

'What a lovely surprise. What time will you be here? Like something special for lunch?'

Zoe couldn't face the thought of food, and she knew she'd need to pinch her cheeks to put some colour in them before she arrived. 'I won't get home until after lunch, Mum. Don't keep anything for me. A cuppa and a couple of biscuits will do.'

'Okay. Look forward to seeing you soon then. Dad will be delighted. We were only talking about you over breakfast this morning and wondering how you were.'

★   ★   ★

As she drove up the narrow approach lane, she was glad to be home at last. She was exhausted and sad and hadn't slept well, but now she was home. She answered her parents' barrage of questions and got up to date with the news about her brother and the rest of the family. Zoe noticed her mother had lots of unspoken questions in her eyes, but sensible as ever, she'd decided not to force any details, and wait for a more auspicious moment. Later Zoe went for a walk around the surrounding fields and felt how she began to relax a little in the familiar location. The sun was setting and a cool wind tugged her hair out of place. The rest of the evening passed without problems.

Later in bed that evening Zoe's father calmed his worried wife and reminded her that Zoe had always trusted in their advice. If she needed it, she'd ask in her own time.

Zoe lay awake for too long as she searched for sleep, but finally her body gave in to pure exhaustion. She woke next morning knowing that Alex had haunted her dreams during the night. Once the crew left, she might eventually feel it was finally finished and over. She lay under the warm duvet and stared up at the sloping ceiling. She could hear her mother busy in the kitchen. The room hadn't been repainted since she'd left her local job to join Williams & Co. in London. That was five years ago. It was a pale yellow with touches of darker gold here and there. It still looked good.

Staring sideways out of the small window set in the eaves, she mused that she was past twenty-five and the only one from her former sixth-form class who wasn't married. It was less likely than ever to happen now. She couldn't imagine ever meeting someone she could love in the same way as she loved Alex. She mused about how many women didn't care about loyalty and commitment. It often looked like many of them were contented with second-best as long as they could have a big wedding and pretend that they'd found a fitting partner, who in reality wasn't fitting at all.

She forced herself to eat a bowl of cornflakes after she got up, just to keep her mother happy. It felt strange to sit in the sunlit kitchen and listen to her mother chatting about the village and people she knew. Her mother had been going to the market day in the next town ever since Zoe could remember. This Thursday was no exception and Zoe agreed to go with her. The hustle and bustle helped to divert her thoughts for a while. They met some neighbours and other people Zoe also knew, and when it was time for the return journey they had overflowing baskets and tit-bits of new information about friends and their families.

Zoe could manage to smile naturally by lunchtime and she felt the tension loosening. Lucy was right. Being in completely different surroundings, with people who loved her, was the best thing she could have done in the circumstances. She'd sent Lucy an SMS to say she'd arrived, but she'd phone her this evening and have a proper chat. After lunch, she insisted on helping her father stack some bales of hay for the winter. It was hard physical work, and she was out of practice, but it felt good to be out in the fresh air doing something useful.

Leaning on a fork and watching him store a bale neatly into place, she said, 'I'm thinking of looking for a new job, Dad.'

'Are you? Trouble at work?'

'No, I like it, but I've been there five years and I need a change.' Zoe stretched her back and leaned on the fork again for a moment. 'Lucy is moving to Scotland soon, and it'll be strange without her. We've always spent most of our spare time together.'

He gave her a gruff laugh. 'Lucy is quite a firework. You two are like fire and water in some ways. She's a good kid underneath though. We like her.'

'Yes, she's a great friend. I'll miss her.' She hoisted another bale upwards and he relieved her of it.

'And what would you like to do? A similar job, or something completely different?'

She waited for him as he stacked the new bale. 'I don't know yet. I haven't started to think about the details. I just feel it's time for a change.'

'You know best. There was an article in the newspaper the other day about your auction house. Did you see it? It was about that treasure hunt in the Caribbean.'

She looked down quickly and then up at him again. 'Yes. I was even with them for a couple of weeks. Not when they actually found the wreck. But . . . I was at the auction too. It went very well. My boss was very pleased, I think.'

'The picture of the crew in the paper was a good one. They look so young.'

Zoe laughed. 'You think anyone under forty is young. Billy would soon put you right about that.' She hastened to explain, 'Billy was the oldest one. He's a gem.'

'Right, pass me another one. They were either lucky or damned clever. It must be like looking for a needle in a haystack if you can believe what the papers say.'

'Very true, but they were lucky and they had a clever leader who knew what he was doing.' She looked around the empty yard. 'I think that's it, Dad. Let's go and have a cup of tea.'

Her father jumped down and threw his arm round her shoulders. 'That's a very good idea.'

★   ★   ★

Zoe phoned Lucy.

'And . . . how are things?'

'You were right to suggest I come home. Being here helps puts things back into perspective. I won't ever forget him, but I realize that I have to live without him and find other things to fill my life.'

'I must say you do sound better, more like your old self again.'

'How did George react when you rang him?'

'He was very understanding. He rambled on about how everyone had been very busy and all the extra work had probably made you susceptible to viruses and bacteria. He didn't even mention you sending a sick note. You have plenty of time to think up an excuse why you haven't been to the doctor's when you get back.'

'And you? Have you done anything about looking for a job in Scotland yet?'

'I've told Andrew I'm willing to give it a try. He seemed really pleased. I know it's easier for me to move than it is for him. He's partner in a firm of lawyers. He'd have to give that up to move to London, and his chances here are completely different than they'd be in Edinburgh.'

'Um! I've started to think about changing my job, too.'

Lucy's voice heightened. 'Really?'

'It seems a good moment. You'll be going, and the auction house will be safe again for a while. This auction will give the company a boost. I need a new challenge.'

Lucy laughed. 'That sounds more like you.'

They talked for a couple of minutes and Zoe promised to call her again as soon as she was back in London.

She spent a comfortable, quiet evening with her parents in front of the television.

★ ★ ★

Next morning the sunshine was at its best. She shared a breakfast with her mother, checked that her father didn't need her help, and then decided to go for a walk up one of the nearby hills. When she was little, after school she'd often gone there with the family dog. She rambled along the slopes and knew all the nooks and crannies. It was her favourite place. Their dog had a wonderful time chasing elusive rabbits, and she'd sat among the waist-high grass weaving daisy-chain necklaces or bracelets. They lived too far away from the village for her to play with her school friends every day, but Zoe didn't mind much. She liked her own company and was never bored.

They didn't have a family dog anymore, but she felt happy as she headed for her favourite spot. It was an outcrop of rock on the other side of the hill, directly behind the house. The weather was good and birds were circling lazily in the blue sky up above. She soon reached her destination and sat down on a piece of rock that overlooked the countryside spreading out before her. The warm wind ruffled her hair. She was dressed in a lightweight jacket, and as she contemplated the scenery she soon found it was too warm and took it off. She made a cushion of it and then stretched out on the rough grass to look up into the blue heaven with its wisps of white clouds.

Lying with her hands behind her head, she was surprised to hear someone crushing the grass as they approached. She looked up and her whole system froze when she saw Alex.

32

She scrambled to a sitting position and felt stunned. Momentarily speechless, she simply stared at him. Idle chatter or a greeting were beyond her capabilities. Seconds passed before she finally managed to say, 'What are you doing here?'

He stood over her, his hands on his hips. 'What are you doing lying there on the side of a hill when you're supposed to be ill?'

'Who told you that?'

'George. He said something about you having flu but I must say, you look remarkably fit if that's true.'

She stuttered slightly. 'It turned out to be a cold. I feel much better already.'

An easy smile played around his mouth. He nodded. 'As I see.'

Still startled, but slowly beginning to accept his presence, she exclaimed, 'I thought you were leaving today. It is Friday today, isn't it?'

He looked at his watch. 'Yes, and the others are leaving in a couple of hours. I wanted to see you first to have a talk.'

As their eyes met, she was amazed at the thrill he gave her. Their words hung in the air among the swishing sound of the grass moving in the wind. She found that her feelings definitely hadn't changed or disintegrated. 'What's so important that you have to come all this way to see me? How did you know where I was?'

'George said you'd gone home. I didn't ask him where your home was, but I asked one of the girls in personnel and she told me, quite discreetly of course.'

Her hopes that she could act with calmness next time she saw him collapsed around her like a house of cards, but the fact that he'd made an effort to come caused a ripple of excitement. It was a heady, potent mixture. 'No doubt you could charm the birds off the trees if you wanted to,' she said. He gave her an infectious grin and sat down next to her. His nearness didn't make the situation easier. 'You haven't explained why you're here.' Zoe had to get it out. 'Oh — congratulations on your engagement.'

His light eyes were startled and wide open as he gazed at her. 'Engagement? What engagement? Mine?'

Brushing some non-existent speck of dirt from her trousers, she looked down. 'Yours and Maria's. I heard her announcing it in the press conference after the auction.'

He threw back his head and chuckled. 'Me and Maria?' He grabbed one of her hands and she tried in vain to wrench it away. 'Maria is engaged to Gary.'

For a moment the air left her lungs and her mind reeled with confusion. 'Maria and Gary? But . . . you and Maria have always been . . . '

He released one hand long enough for him to place a finger over her lips.

She had an urge to kiss it, but she didn't.

Almost triumphantly, he gazed at her and uttered, 'Damn it! Billy was right.'

'Pardon? What are you talking about?' She tried again to free her hand but he held on until he suddenly slipped his hands round her shoulders instead. She was forced to face him. She could see the white lines at the corners of his eyes and his enticing lips just centimetres away. She could smell his skin and study his features. She thought she'd never see him again, and here he was with her, on the hill above her parents' farm. He felt so big, so safe, so masculine and hard.

'Let's get one thing straight. I was never close to Maria in that way.'

Weakly she replied, 'Never?'

'No, I've never thought about Maria in a romantic way.'

'But you — you and her . . . on board ship . . .'

He sighed quietly. 'Let's begin at the beginning. I worked together with

Maria's father on a rig a couple of years ago. We became friends and then eventually we both moved on to other jobs. He had a family and eventually opened a small boatyard because he wanted to settle down.'

It was impossible for Zoe to do anything but look into his dear face, and she nodded silently. She noticed how his neck was beautifully tanned to the colour of toffee, and she had an absurd longing to taste it.

Smiling a wicked slow smile that caught her unaware somewhere in the middle of her stomach, he went on, 'Sanchez and I kept in touch. When I was in the vicinity, he invited me around and I got to know his relatives. They're a warm-hearted, cheerful family and everything seemed perfect. One day I heard that Maria had married a scientist. He was studying sea algae and working at a research institution near San Diego. Fine, I thought, next time you visit them you'll have to remember to buy her a wedding present.

'Out of the blue one day, Sanchez got in touch again. By then I was already making plans for the treasure hunt, and people I knew had spread the word. That was just before you must have heard about the hunt from Tony. Sanchez asked me to call, so I did. When I got round to visiting them, Maria was at home. I noticed straight away that she looked bad. She was thin, pale, and silent. She was completely unlike the Maria I knew from earlier times. I didn't like that because she was the sister I never had.'

Zoe started to say something but he shook his head. 'Let me finish, and then you can ask as much as you like.' She listened, half in anticipation and half in dread.

'Sanchez explained that Maria's husband had turned out to be a kind of Jekyll-and-Hyde. He seemed sociable and likeable, but he had two faces. One of those faces wasn't very pleasant, and it was the one he assumed when he was together with his wife. When they first married everything was okay, but then he grew over-possessive and jealous, and had outbursts of violent temper. He created scenes at her workplace with her fellow workers, and it was so bad and embarrassing that in the end she quit. Then he started to accuse her of laziness, and kept urging her to find a job. She tried, but nothing she found in the newspapers or elsewhere suited him, and he wouldn't even allow her to submit an application. He turned into a control freak and finally started to get physically violent with her.'

With wide eyes, Zoe managed to interrupt him long enough to ask, 'Why didn't she get help? She had a family. Or she could have gone to the authorities if she didn't want to involve them.'

He studied her face silently. 'Apparently, often women who are in this sort of situation think at first that it's just a momentary slip-up and won't happen again. The culprit shows remorse and promises to change, but he doesn't. As time goes on, the women are too embarrassed to tell anyone what's wrong and by then the men have forced them to cut any social contacts. If there are children involved, it's even more complicated. The women are too confused and shocked to find their own way out. They don't realize a telephone call or a visit to a suitable organization might give them the chance of a new start.'

'Is that what Maria did to escape his clutches?'

He shook his head. 'Sanchez visited Maria unexpectedly one day and found her with a black eye and bruises. When she told him what had been going on, Sanchez waited until her husband came home. Then he beat him up. Sanchez broke his nose and gave him a shattered kneecap.' Alex grinned and continued. 'He took Maria home. Maria got a divorce, but it didn't end there. He started stalking her. Maria couldn't go anywhere without him turning up. In the end, a court order declared he was not allowed to go within a mile, and later five miles, of where she was. The terror continued — telephone calls, anonymous letters and emails, and despite the court order the occasional sighting. Maria was frightened and Sanchez wanted her out of the way. He asked me to take her along on the search.' Alex paused for a moment. 'That was roughly when you came into my life.

'I told the rest of the crew about Maria. She'd already reverted to her maiden name to cover her tracks. We'd agreed it was best to keep her history a secret from anyone we came in contact with, to reduce the risk he'd find her. She knew about diving and all the technicalities, so she fitted in well. When you came on board we kept you in the dark to be sure you wouldn't say something to the wrong person. It would have been more sensible to tell you the truth outright. We soon decided you were no blabbermouth. By the time I decided it was a stupid idea not to have told you the truth, you had Maria and me paired up and I never got the chance to explain. We expected Maria's husband would have a very hard job to find her. Once we were at sea, she was out of reach and he wouldn't be able to see her. But we underestimated his determination . . . He was so mad, he never gave up searching. Finally he engaged a couple of ruffians who owned a run-down boat to kidnap her.'

She was startled. 'Are you talking about the men who kidnapped us?'

He nodded. 'Bingo! I thought they were following us because of the treasure, but they were after Maria.'

'But they took me too!'

'That wasn't part of the arrangement. You just got in the way so they took you too.'

'Did they intend to turn Maria over to him?'

'That seems to have been the plan.'

'And what then? He couldn't keep her by force, could he? Not forever.'

He loosened his hold and stroked the

hair out of her face. 'Sometimes people are held against their will for years, sometimes forever. A stranger moves into a town somewhere, keeps himself to himself, and never invites anyone to his home. It's easier than one imagines.'

'And me?'

'We'll never know. You'd probably seen too much for them to let you go.'

Feeling shocked, she considered him for a moment. He could see the alarm in her face and he pulled her to him. She felt the heady sensation of his lips on hers. It left her with increased desire. He came to his feet in a fluid moment, and pulled her up with him. His hands explored the soft lines of her waist and her hips. Their closeness was lulling her into a state of euphoria. His lips recaptured hers and were more demanding. She gave in to the heady sensation. The flame of desire between them should have surprised her, but it didn't.

He let out an audible sigh. Gazing at her, he kissed the tip of her nose and said, 'I never thought anyone would ever make me feel like this.' His gaze made explanations unnecessary. Zoe found it hard to think sensibly.

'What happened to the ex-husband?'

'They caught one of the crooks who kidnapped you both, and he tried to lessen his own blame by accusing the others. Then they caught the leader and through him, Maria's husband. He was still in the process of selling their house in San Diego to pay for Maria's abduction and whatever he planned for later. When the case gets to court, he'll face a tough sentence. Maria and Gary fell for each other during the trip. They plan to open a diving school.'

Breathlessly she murmured, 'Yes, she mentioned Hawaii at the press conference, didn't she?' She couldn't keep her eyes off his lips and wished desperately that he'd kiss her again.

He shook his head. 'They'll end up somewhere else. They decided to lay a false trail. From what I gather, Maria's whole family is planning to uproot and cut all connections with the past, so that even if her ex-husband gets out years from now he'll have a hell of a job to find out where anyone is. They're proposing to set up a business in a warm climate — Australia, the Philippines, or the South Seas. There's even talk of them staying in the Caribbean, because he's less likely to believe they'd stay put.' He ran his finger down the side of her face. 'Thank heavens he's behind bars.'

'How long do you think he'll be there?'

Alex shrugged. 'In some states in America he'd get the death penalty, but I should imagine that unless he has a very clever lawyer, the least he'll get is a life sentence. The length of that varies from place to place, but kidnapping is never a minor offence.'

'Will I have to give evidence?' She let her thoughts ramble. 'Heavens! My parents don't even know I was involved. They'll go crazy when I tell them!'

He laughed softly. 'I'll help, if you let

me. I just talked to your mother briefly and she knew who I was from the newspaper reports. I think she's already putting two and two together, now I've turned up on their doorstep.'

She looked at him and swallowed the lump in her throat. 'I bet she is. Even if I was wrong about you and Maria, you still have a history of loving and leaving. That's not what I want. I don't want a fast and meaningless affair that goes nowhere.'

He pulled her swiftly into his arms and kissed her roughly. 'Would I be here if I just wanted a quick affair?' He held her at arm's length. 'I understand why you feel that way, but I swear I've never felt like this before in my whole life. I felt so helpless when we found someone had kidnapped you, along with Maria. I was already in love with you by then. I realized you'd judged the situation wrongly, but I couldn't break my word to Sanchez and tell you about Maria until the others all agreed. I thought I'd have time.

'When we rescued you I wanted to grab you, but Maria grabbed me first. I saw the reaction in your face and it gave me hope, but then everything went haywire and you pushed me away. You didn't know the truth about Maria or that I was in love with you. And after you left with the police I wondered if I'd had the wrong impression. Billy kept telling me I was a fool not to find out where we stood.'

'And what about the past girlfriends?'

He smiled and held her tighter. She could feel the hard contours of his body. 'Dear heart, compared to what I feel for you, they mean nothing to me. And before you accuse me of being heartless, I never pretended I was looking for a serious relationship with any of them. They knew and accepted me for what I was.' Tilting his head, he said, 'You may be surprised to know that there are lots of women who are also merely interested in a dead-end affair. Not everyone is like my green-eyed goddess who is determined to wait for someone she can trust and count on. I'm hoping that you'll give me the chance to prove I'm the one for you. We have something special between us and it's been there from that first evening in London. We both feel it, so don't try to deny it. You resisted me from the word go, didn't you? You put a lot of energy into running away from me. There is a much better way to use that energy. Do I have a chance?'

It was so easy to agree. She nodded. 'I can't help it. I don't know why it had to be you. Even though I believed you wanted Maria, it didn't stop me falling in love with you.'

His smile was wide and approving. 'I promise I'm not going to steamroller you into anything. We'll get to know each other properly. We've lost too much time dodging each other, haven't we? Now we'll build a real relationship and take our time.'

With an eager smile, she gave in. Love was confusing and scary, but she loved him. If he wanted her as much as she wanted him, it was worth trying. 'That sounds wonderful. What do you intend to do now, apart from concentrating on me? Salvage work? Another search?'

'Nothing that keeps us apart. The search was a lucky one. We can all afford to lean back now and concentrate on something else. At the moment, my main interest is confined to what's good for you and me. Perhaps I'll go for something completely different. Something that's just as enjoyable.'

She couldn't believe he was so close, and that he wanted her as much as she wanted him. She stared at him with longing and then reached up and touched the side of his face with her fingers. He turned his head and kissed her fingertips and her heart turned over. Sounding sensible but feeling unbelievably buoyant, she said, 'Like what?'

'It would be fun to manage a marina somewhere with a decent climate. In Spain perhaps, or somewhere in the

Caribbean. I could even teach marine engineering. I've enough practical experience and I'm qualified. It all depends on you, on what you want to do.'

'On me?' A feeling like lightening travelled across her system as she gazed at him, and she tried to smother it in more sensible feelings. She was unsuccessful.

'Of course, we'll decide things together from now on. We'll choose things that make both of us feel useful and happy.'

As well as a sense of euphoria, she could only muse that it was incredible.

He looked at her and said softly, 'You have to learn to trust me. I love you. I can't give you a guarantee that there'll be no bumps along the way, but I'll do my damndest to smooth our road. We'll start by building on what we already have — our feelings. I've never felt anything similar before in my life. We've been apart more than we've been together, but that hasn't stopped me wanting and thinking about you the whole time. That tells me a lot about myself, and how strongly I feel for you. I'm sure you're the one for me. I hope you'll give us a chance. Will you?'

He was all she wanted. Why did she think for a single moment that she was strong enough to walk away? Not now, and not ever. He'd said he loved her; that was the kind of bliss she wanted. She felt happy and alive, and she knew she had to trust him to give their love a chance; she did now. She nodded. 'Of course.' She drank in the sweetness of his kiss and wished it would never end. Her limbs felt warm and heavy, and there was a tingling inside that flared and grew into blatant desire.

33

Zoe stood at the railings in shorts and a T-shirt. The others were crowded on the narrow causeway, offering unwanted advice and suggestive proposals.

Alex laughed at their good-natured jesting. 'It's about time we left. They're only delaying us. We don't need all these lewd suggestions. We have enough imagination and ideas of our own.'

Zoe looked at them. Gary and Maria looking contented and happy. Hank had his little girl on his shoulder and his arm around his wife. Billy had pushed his hat low on his brow to shut out the sun. They all continued to shout at them and laugh.

They'd married in the UK and had a traditional wedding with Lucy as a flamboyant chief bridesmaid. They agreed that it would be nice to celebrate with the crew before they left on their honeymoon, cruising around the Caribbean islands. Alex had had several offers for the boat, but decided to keep it. Billy agreed to be its caretaker when they weren't using it.

★   ★   ★

Alex kissed her briefly and turned away. His kiss was accompanied by whistling and hooting and he grinned broadly on his way to the bridge. Billy freed the mooring ropes and Alex revved the engine and guided the *Astrea* into deeper waters. Zoe waved until they were all mere silhouettes in the distance. She still couldn't believe her luck and the happiness she now felt. She hurried to join him as they drew further and further away from the pier.

He pulled her close and nuzzled her neck. 'I can't believe it. We've made it and I've got you to myself at last. We're on our way to the best time of our lives at last, I hope.' His eyes twinkled for a moment. 'That's as long as you don't get seasick again!'

We do hope that you have enjoyed reading this large print book.

Did you know that all of our titles are available for purchase?

We publish a wide range of high quality large print books including:
**Romances, Mysteries, Classics
General Fiction
Non Fiction and Westerns**

Special interest titles available in large print are:
**The Little Oxford Dictionary
Music Book, Song Book
Hymn Book, Service Book**

Also available from us courtesy of Oxford University Press:
**Young Readers' Dictionary
(large print edition)
Young Readers' Thesaurus
(large print edition)**

For further information or a free brochure, please contact us at:
**Ulverscroft Large Print Books Ltd.,
The Green, Bradgate Road, Anstey,
Leicester, LE7 7FU, England.
Tel:** (00 44) 0116 236 4325
Fax: (00 44) 0116 234 0205